Guardian Angel: True Calling

Brian D. Campbell

To Jim
Thanks again for your excellent work and honest feedback. Hope to work with you again.
Brian Campbell

Printed in the United States of America
First Printing, 2019

ISBN 978-1-7329161-3-5 (Paperback)
ISBN 978-1-7329161-4-2 (Mobi eBook)

Red Cliff Press
PO Box 371
New Boston, NH 03070

Dedicated to Renee Campbell

None of this is possible, or

nearly as fun, without you.

Prologue
Winter of 1784 - Boston, Massachusetts
From the Memoir of Colonel Oliver Deerfield

Our spies told us the British were preparing to march from the city, out into the hills, to take and fortify those positions overlooking Boston. Colonel William Prescott gathered some thousand militiamen and hurried from Cambridge to the vacant hills.

We fortified the land as best we could out of earth and waited for the red-coated bastards. Our orders were to fortify Bunker Hill, but our commanding officers thought it wise to station ourselves on the smaller Breed's Hill. Breed's Hill is closer to the city, with less ground to cover. This helped our inferior numbers appear stronger, though some in my company feared being in close proximity to British artillery.

We had a gentleman in our company, a doctor, rumored to be an officer of significant rank. Perhaps even a major general, though he fought at my side as if he were a private, like I was at this the early stage of the war. He didn't give any orders. He fought like a lion and inspired us to follow him. And we did, instinctively.

The British set Charlestown ablaze, just below Breed's Hill, and pounded our modest fortifications with cannon fire before they advanced. The intense heat from the fire and the roaring cannons tested our resolve, but we stood our ground.

The redcoats advanced once toward our earthworks and we did as our commanders instructed. "Hold your fire until the bastards are within fifty yards of our lines."

We stopped them, inflicting many casualties. But they regrouped and advanced a second time. After we punished them again, inflicting even more casualties than before, they retreated away from our fortifications.

We learned something about the enemy's resolve that day, as they assembled yet again to attempt a third assault. I, like most of the men around me, had nothing left to fire at them during their third advance. I meant to run before they fired a volley and overran our position, to slaughter us all.

I prepared myself to bolt into the country, but I saw the doctor-gentleman stand his ground, ready to fight a thousand men alone, throwing rocks and swinging his musket, so the rest of us could get away. He kept yelling at us to run, as the enemy charged with bayonet, and many of the men did. Most who stayed to fight were brutally defeated.

"Save yourselves! Fight another day!"

I couldn't leave him there to die alone, so I stood next to him and accepted his fate as my own while militiamen ran off in every direction.

When the fighting was nearly over, and only a few Colonials remained standing, I watched in horror as a British officer calmly approach our position with pistol drawn. "Dr. Joseph Warren. What an honor it is to make your acquaintance."

The officer pointed his weapon at Dr. Warren's head and fired into his face, killing him where he stood. The British stripped his corpse and stabbed it all over, tossing it into a shallow grave with another unfortunate patriot who had fallen moments before.

Dr. Warren could only be recognized by his wooden teeth, which were crafted by Paul Revere, the same man who later identified the major general.

By the grace of God, I escaped that terrible scene with my life.

A short time later, I learned more about Dr. Joseph Warren. He was indeed a major general, but with no fighting experience. Because of that, he insisted to General Israel Putman that he be allowed to fight as a private. He requested to be stationed where the heaviest fighting might take place. And he did fight. And he did inspire men to fight with him.

I will never forget my short time at Major General Warren's side. How many men would give such a magnificent life so freely? So that a company of men like me, in dirty rags, with hardly more than nothing, could live. So that we could fight another day and claim an impossible victory against a far superior opponent. A victory that would give birth to the greatest nation on God's Earth. A nation where men like me were held in the same regard as kings and men like Dr. Joseph Warren. From my time at Breed's Hill, until the end of the war, my resolve to fight remained steadfast.

God keep and rest Dr. Joseph Warren. Patriot. Son of Liberty.

Chapter 1

Billy Sullivan, wearing an expensive tailored suit, his dark hair slicked straight back like a man who had no time for styling, paced impatiently next to his father's hospital bed, waving his arms and shouting.

"He just quit. He left town and ran back to Arkansas with his tail between his legs. And the old man *still* made him Worshipful Master of the Brothers of Herrad. That's your job. Oh, and then the old man gave him a pile of money to start some club for underprivileged kids. In the middle of nowhere!" Billy yelled, completely unaware of how serious the prognosis was for his father.

Bradford Sullivan waited patiently for his son to calm down so he could inform him that he wouldn't be leaving the University of Kansas Cancer Center alive.

The older man had spent months ignoring his discomfort and then waited even longer, until he could no longer tolerate the pain, to see a doctor. By then, the cancer that started in his pancreas had spread all over his body. He'd been informed, before Billy arrived, that no treatment available could save him. The hospital could only offer to make his final days less painful.

Bradford sighed, "I don't know why you're still paying any attention to the Brothers of Herrad, or Ben Gilsum. All of that's in the past now."

"Dad, that little bastard took *everything* from us. I'll tell you what *I* don't know. *I* don't know how you can just let it all go so easily!"

"Son, please stop yelling for a moment. I have something far more important to tell you. Why don't you sit for a minute and calm down?"

Billy did as his father asked and flopped down in a chair beside the bed, still simmering. He looked up at the ceiling, clearly irritated, exhaled loudly, and then lowered his gaze to his father. "OK, I'm calm. What have you got to tell me?"

"Good. Focus on what I'm about to say now, and please try to control your temper. Don't get angry. Don't start yelling again. There are very sick people around us who would appreciate some quiet rest. Do as I ask, and don't argue."

Bradford let out a feeble moan, and pushed the button on his pain-relief system. "I'm dying, William. I have days, not months." He kept talking, not allowing his son to interrupt. "I've arranged to have all of our finances merged into one account. You have it all now. Everything we earned in Washington, DC is yours. You're a very wealthy man."

"How is this possible?" Billy spoke over his father, beginning to yell again. "They said it was treatable. Didn't they? You're supposed to be out of here in a few days." He stood back up and pounded on the wall of the hospital room in defiance.

"Quiet down, Son," Bradford demanded. "I want you to forget about that, and everything else. The Brothers of Herrad, the old man, his grandson, and especially your obsession with Ben Gilsum. Leave me here to rot and go back to Boston. Spend some time with your mother. She misses you terribly. Don't come back out here and don't attempt any more dealings with Doug Tamworth. You're not ready for that. And I'm not going to be around to teach you anything else. Take the money and live a long, happy life. Promise me, and then go."

Billy didn't speak for a few moments. He looked down, closed his eyes tight, raised a shaking, clenched fist close to his face, and then lowered his hand quickly, opening his palm as if he were tossing something away.

He began pacing again, silently this time, staring at his father in disbelief. *He just wants me to give up? He doesn't think I can make it without him?*

The young man shook his head, full of rage. *I'm supposed to forget all about Ben Gilsum? Just let that asshole walk? And I can handle whatever that weasel, Doug Tamworth, has in mind without help from my daddy.*

Billy stopped pacing and took a deep breath. "Dad, I promise." He spoke the words, but knew he'd made a promise he'd never be able to keep. His father knew it, too.

"I don't know what else to say. You want me to just walk away from you like this? Leave you here, to die alone?" Billy found it impossible to hide his anger.

"Yes. That's exactly what I want," Bradford declared. "And promise me one more time that you'll do the other things I've asked."

"OK, Dad. I promise."

Billy turned his back to his father and walked out of the room without speaking another word. He realized he would never see him again. A few tears fell from his eyes, but they were coming more from rage than sorrow. *We came out here from DC to get back into the game after that rat, Ben Gilsum, ruined everything. I'll go back east, Dad. I'll go home, to Boston. But I'm not leaving here until Ben Gilsum pays!*

Chapter 2

Fall in Decatur, Arkansas felt much cooler than Ben Gilsum remembered. He'd been away from home for just two years, but everything seemed new. The morning air felt crisp as he and his father made their way to work at the plant in Mr. Gilsum's old pickup truck. The two men made an odd pair—a handsome young man, dressed in business-casual attire, which included a slim-fit suit, fitted dress shirt, and expensive leather shoes, and a much older and weather-beaten man, with hard-earned wrinkles, dressed in denim overalls and a worn-out old t-shirt.

The tall, dark, and attractive young man stared out the passenger-side window, admiring the mixture of red and green leaves as they passed the abandoned old church building he had recently acquired. The same building would become his home in the coming weeks.

Several days had passed since the younger Gilsum began advertising to build interest for the Decatur Club for Boys and Girls, which would also be housed at the old church. The town seemed remarkably receptive to the young man's plans and he already had a few sponsors lined up.

Notorious in Decatur for his crippling-shy demeanor, the attractive and well-spoken young man became energized and electric while discussing his vision. Everyone he spoke to about the project could sense his passion. And the fact that he had plenty of funding made it easier to offer their support. There was still a great deal of work to do and equipment to buy in order to set things up the way he envisioned, but he planned to open the doors before the start of the New Year.

Ben felt happy to be home; his mother's health was declining rapidly due to muscular dystrophy, and he wanted to spend more time with her before things got worse. While anxious to get out of his parents' house again, the distance between them would only be a few miles this time.

"Dad, there's something I want to talk to you about," Ben said, coming back from his vision of the future for the old church. The building was recently gifted to him by a ridiculously wealthy and dear friend he knew back in DC, along with a substantial donation to "cover the operating expenses for a while."

His father kept his eyes on the road and replied, "Mmm-hmm."

"I've been in contact with John Brown University. I applied for a job there as an Associate Professor in the history department and they called me in for an interview."

Mr. Gilsum gave another "Mmm-hmm," and kept his eyes forward, appearing unfazed.

Disappointed by the lack of interest his father seemed to be showing, Ben paused awhile before adding, "I just wanted to let you know that I may be leaving the plant if they offer me a job at John Brown. I didn't wanna leave without telling you first."

Mr. Gilsum picked up on his son's frustration and finally began to speak. "Son, I've been workin' at the plant for how long now? Some forty years, I guess. They've been good to me, too."

Ben looked at his father, happy to finally get an actual reaction from him.

Mr. Gilsum continued, "There's two things I learned workin' at the plant this long. One, it's honest work and they take good care of this town. T'other is you don't belong there. You never did belong there."

Mr. Gilsum turned to his only child. "You go take that job at John Brown. And know I'm proud of you, don't matter what you do. But you belong in a place like John Brown University and not at some old chicken processing plant out here in the sticks of Northwest Arkansas."

Moved by his father's rare show of emotion, the young man replied, "Well, it's a good job, and I'll have to go back to school, too. I'm gonna need a master's degree, and maybe even a PhD if I want to advance. I'm excited about it," Ben declared. "But listen, they haven't offered me anything yet, so this is between you and me. Apparently the head of the history department knows someone from back in DC, maybe someone I worked with there,

I don't know. I'll find out who that is when I go in for the interview. Networking pays off I guess, even here in Decatur."

Mr. Gilsum, exhausted from showing a little emotion, went back to his prior reply, "Mmm-hmm," as a mischievous smile appeared on the older man's tired and weather-beaten face.

"What are you thinking about over there, Dad? Let's hear it, old man."

"Well, you know they got a lot of fine universities back east? Say somewheres near Boston? Isn't that where your Angel is?" Mr. Gilsum couldn't help himself and Ben hadn't told his parents anything about what had happened back in Virginia. They still believed Angelina Rindge was the right match for their son based on how much he changed, for the better, since they first heard about her. In their mind, Angelina transformed their shy and awkward son into a confident and charming man.

"Dad, you know Patty's coming for a visit in three weeks, right?"

"Oh yeah, that's right. The *other* girl from Washington, DC. The one who went and booked a room at the Wingate Hotel over in Bentonville, some fifteen miles away. I betcha your Angel woulda gone and smacked some sense into you if you'd tried to pull that one with her. She'd be stayin' with us in Decatur for sure. She's a good girl, Son."

One of these days I'm going to have to set them straight about Angel. Just not today.

Ben didn't bother to say any more about it. When he booked the room for his long-distance girlfriend, Patty, he planned to tell his parents he chose the hotel because of its convenient location, just two miles north of the airport. He quickly realized they wouldn't buy that, so he didn't try.

Patty knew Ben had grown up in poverty, and his parents still lived a humble life. Ben knew she didn't care, but he wasn't ready for her to stay at their house longer than it took to have dinner and perhaps a desert, a rarity reserved for special occasions at the Gilsum house.

Still contemplating how Patty's visit would go, knowing his parents unfairly hated her, Ben caught a glimpse of a familiar car passing them at a high rate of speed from the other direction. A dark-blue Mercedes S-Class Sedan. The same car he had seen weeks earlier while on his way to become the new owner of the old church. He stopped his daydreaming and tried to turn and find it, but it was gone.

"Dad, did you see that car?"

"Woo, yeah. Prettiest car I ever saw in Decatur. 'Cept maybe that one the feller drove that you got the old church from. Course that one had an unfortunate brown color to it. This new feller must be in some kinda hurry, though, like a shiny blue flash flyin' down the road."

"Did you happen to see the license plate? Was it out of state?"

Mr. Gilsum laughed. "No, Perry Mason, I didn't catch that. You want I should turn around and chase him down in this here old Chevy?"

It can't be. Why would he be here?

Chapter 3

Spring of 2007 - Wellesley, Massachusetts

"What on Earth has happened to your clothes, Angelina?" Deanne Rindge shouted at her nine-year-old daughter, who stood before her mother looking tattered. She and her twin brother Alex had tried to sneak into the house to get cleaned up, before their mother saw them, after a Saturday morning playing outside.

Deanne Rindge appeared to be much younger than a mother with nine-year-old twins, though she was only thirty. She was tall, with short brown-wavy hair and dark blue eyes, elegant and well respected in the family's up-scale neighborhood.

The twins were completely different in appearance and personality. No one ever believed they were siblings. Both children were bright, straight A students, but that's where the similarities ended. Alex was a bookworm with very few friends. He was a small, timid child who quickly turned away when anyone spoke to him. For years he clung to his mother's side and cried if anyone looked at him.

Angelina stood four inches taller than her brother, wild, full of energy and the most popular girl at school. She was athletic and already a star on her travel basketball team.

The twins stood side by side as their mother interrogated them.

"And you, Alex. My goodness. You look like you've been rolled around in the dirt like a rag doll. Is that blood on your arm?"

Alex began to cry as he looked at the back of his wrist, which he had used to wipe his bloody nose a few moments ago. "I don't know, Mom," was all he could manage.

"Bob, get in here and look at your children!" Deanne shouted to the air, hoping to get their father's attention.

Robert Rindge made his way through the beautiful 9,500 square-foot home in Wellesley, Massachusetts. He was fit and tan. Robert was shorter and several years older than his wife. He was dressed in knickers and tall white socks that met them just below his knees. That, along with his white polo shirt meant he was ready to hit the links with some very powerful politicians and didn't have much time to inspect his children before heading out.

"What the heck happened to you two?" Robert asked with a chuckle as he looked them over.

Alex was still sobbing, staring at the floor. Angelina stood firm, looking her father in the eyes. She knew once Daddy appeared on the scene she wasn't going to be punished if she showed him how spirited and strong she was.

"Well, Angel, spill it. I don't have time to spare. What happened?"

"Donnie Chalet beat up Alex again," Angelina said calmly. She became more excited with the rest of her confession. "He's always picking on Alex. I warned him last time that I was gonna pound on him if he didn't stop hurting my brother."

Angelina calmed down, maintained her posture, and made eye contact again with her father. "Well, he didn't stop, Daddy. So I beat him up. He grabbed my shirt and it ripped after I punched him and knocked him down."

"And then he ran home, crying to his *mama,*" a proud Alex announced, no longer crying, adding his favorite part to the confession.

Mr. Rindge bit his lip, trying not to expose his smile, and looked at his wife who was still angry at her children and now angry at her husband for encouraging their only daughter to fight. It was Mr. Rindge, after all, who had told Angelina and Alex the only way to stop a bully was to punch them in the nose as hard as you could.

Robert shrugged at his wife and looked at his watch. "Honey, I need to get going. Now.

"Look, gang, I wish I had more time to discuss this with you, but I'm meeting someone for golf who could be our next senator. And I'm late. Kids, we'll talk about this later, OK? Over ice cream,

Angel?" the proud father asked, beaming as he messed up his daughter's hair.

"Don't worry, Bob, your future senator will wait for you. As long as the donations keep coming, he'll wait for you," an annoyed Mrs. Rindge added, turning her head, offering only a cheek for him to kiss goodbye before he made his way to the door.

Before Robert could open the door and exit, the bell rang. An angry Fred Chalet stood next to his miserable son Donnie on the front porch, in the way of Robert who was only steps away from making his typical Saturday escape to the golf course.

"Robert, I'd like to talk with you about your daughter. Look at my son's face," Fred demanded. "I expect there to be an apology in the least, followed by some severe form of punishment. Wouldn't you agree?"

Mr. Rindge looked at his watch and couldn't hide how annoyed he'd become at being late for his tee time with the future senator.

"Sure, Fred. When Donald's ready to tell Alex he's sorry for the months of torment and beatings he's been giving him, we're ready to accept his apology. Happily. Oh, and however you decide to discipline your son is none of my business. Good day, Fred. I'm late for something far more important than this."

Chapter 4

"Soderquest Business Center, room 233," Ben said aloud to himself, while driving his Jeep Wrangler to John Brown University.

The Jeep was his first purchase after graduating from JBU and taking a job in Washington, DC as an Intelligence Analyst. It was his reward to himself for escaping a lifetime of poverty, his way to make up for the confidence-crushing pain that it brought. Driving his Jeep and either talking to himself about whatever was weighing on his mind or singing along with the radio was Ben's method for managing stress.

Two and a half years had passed since Ben last visited his alma mater. The standout math and history graduate was heavily recruited and quickly whisked away to the nation's capital. That felt like a lifetime ago.

"Dr. Gregory Orchard, chair of the history department, and Dr. Prichard Gross, Dean of Undergraduate Studies. I know Dr. Orchard pretty well, he likes me. Or at least he did when I aced all his classes," the nervous interviewee declared, trying to boost his confidence as he reminded himself of the names of his interviewers.

"OK, here goes nothing. Time to make my first vacation day from the plant count." Ben announced as he made his way to Soderquest Business Center.

The campus at John Brown University didn't look any different than it did two and a half years prior. There weren't many people walking around at 7:00 AM and it was cold outside. *I don't remember Arkansas being this cold.*

The private Christian college looked clean and beautiful, just like Ben remembered, with a mixture of modern buildings and cathedral structures. The sun had just started to peek over half-bare trees that clung to the last of their red leaves while the rest were swirling around with the steady wind over the still-green grass. *I do love a college campus in the fall. Man, I want this job.*

"There's my favorite Early American History student," Dr. Orchard shouted as Ben made his way to the front door of the Soderquest Business Center. "How have you been, Mr. Gilsum? It's nice to see you."

Dr. Gregory Orchard was a tall, thin man. At six feet, six inches he towered over Ben who was just over six feet. Dr. Orchard had a full head of gray hair, neatly parted on one side, not a strand out of place. He was friendly, energetic, and his students loved his classes because of his enthusiasm for the subject and demeanor. He was Ben's favorite person at JBU, and the two men had quickly become fond of each other, but lost touch after Ben took the job in DC.

"Dr. Orchard, thank you so much for agreeing to see me about the…"

"It's my absolute pleasure," Gregory Orchard interrupted. "Feel a little strange being on campus again, now that you're a graduate who's seen the world?"

"Feels great actually. I forgot how much I loved this place in the fall."

"It's pretty, isn't it? Well, Dr. Gross is waiting for us inside. He's new, Ben; he doesn't know you. But I've told him how gifted a student and how terrific a citizen you were while attending class here. He's anxious to meet you."

The men made their way inside to a conference room at the Business Center where the department head liked to conduct interviews and meetings.

Dr. Prichard Gross, a man just into his sixties, short and bald with a plaid sports coat he couldn't button over his belly, stood up to welcome them.

"You must be our young Mr. Gilsum," Dr. Gross said as they shook hands. "It's a pleasure to meet you."

"Likewise, Dr. Gross. I'm thankful to be here, Sir."

"I'm going to be conducting the interview today, and Dr. Gross will observe. We're going to be here a while, the room was supposed to be catered with coffee and donuts, but it's still early. Perhaps they'll be along shortly," Dr. Orchard predicted. "We'll have lunch here, too, most likely, and then we'll turn you loose. You ready to get started?"

"Absolutely, and again I'm really thankful for you inviting me to be here…"

Dr. Orchard interrupted again, "OK, so the first thing we need to talk about is what we're looking for. We need another teacher in the history department. I've begun taking on more administrative responsibilities and no longer have the bandwidth to maintain a full course load. The job posting is for an Associate Professor, which implies an experienced candidate."

Dr. Orchard paused and looked at Dr. Gross before proceeding. "Ben, to be frank, you don't have the typical qualifications we look for in a teaching candidate. This would be a highly unusual hire for us. Sure, you're gifted. As a student you were second to none, probably the best student I've ever had. Before the company came in and stole you from us, I wanted to offer you a job here. But my plan was to start you out as an Assistant Professor while you earned your master's and teaching credentials. And though we posted for an Associate Professor, we might be open to filling our needs with an Assistant Professor, should we find the right person."

"I understand," Ben said. "I intend to get back to the classroom myself. I can earn a master's in a year if I work hard. I'm also going to go on to a PhD if that's needed down the road."

"I think that's the right idea," Dr. Orchard said, exchanging looks again with Dr. Gross. "We've never hired an Assistant Professor without a master's degree. As you know, this university has a very prestigious reputation. All of our professors are well known in their field. In order to advance here, all of them have been published or recognized with awards, preferably both. Hiring you could cause a stir among our faculty."

Ben looked down, discouraged, as he listened to his old professor's words. *Where have I heard this before?* This was the same type of discussion he'd had during his interview with his former boss at the company back in Washington, DC. "We never hire a kid fresh out of college to be an Intelligence Analyst."

"Don't let any of this worry you. We intend to give you the opportunity to prove you're worthy. And I'm excited about that," Dr. Orchard added. "Your selection for an interview may be odd, but that doesn't disqualify you. You're a rare find, Mr. Gilsum. The amount of knowledge and enthusiasm you possess for American History is extremely uncommon for a person your age. That's why you're here."

"I'd like to second what Dr. Orchard just said," Dr. Gross added, trying to reassure Ben that it was more than his colleague's fondness of him that got him the interview. "I've discussed your achievements with many of your professors and they've all agreed with Dr. Orchard's assessment. I'm not sure many would object to you joining us, especially those who know you. And if the others do, they can take that up with me or the president of the university. She likes you, too," Dr. Gross added with a wink.

The interview began with a series of scripted questions, meant to assess the candidate's enthusiasm for teaching, temperament, knowledge, and background, most of which would be researched outside of the conference room. Since Ben had a short resume, and his interviewer knew him so well, this was a painless process, though it took two hours to get through.

The next exercise caught Ben off guard. Though he thought he came fully prepared, he missed a key element of a typical interview for a college professor.

"This is my favorite part of these interviews," Dr. Orchard said. "Dr. Gross and I are going to relax a bit. I'm going to stop talking, and you're going to give us a lesson. It can be any topic, doesn't even have to be history. Lecture us, Professor Gilsum. Teach me something. Let's see what you've got."

The normally well-prepared young man wanted to kick himself for not realizing, or researching, that there would be a teaching demonstration involved with his interview. *How could I have been so naïve?*

Though his mind was racing, Ben refused to allow himself to panic. A smile came to his face as he thought of the time, a few months before leaving DC, when his girlfriend invited him to come with her and visit her parents in Boston.

"Before we discuss one of my favorite accounts of the Revolutionary War, I'd like to share a story with you about my one and only visit to Boston. Our gracious hosts, my girlfriend's parents, offered to take us anywhere in the city we chose during our last afternoon in town, before we made our way back to Washington, DC, where we both lived at the time. I immediately thought of the Henry Knox Trail, and insisted we go there. The final marker along the trail from Upstate New York to Boston was only a few miles away and I was excited to see it. No one else had ever heard of it, so my chance to shine, right? Well, that marker is nothing more than a lonely, engraved stone in an empty park, and needless to say, I was the only one excited about the activities that afternoon. My travel companions were bored stiff. No brownie points for me that day.

"So what is the Henry Knox Trail, and why was I so excited to see it? In 1775, young Major General Henry Knox was assigned an impossible task by General George Washington. Knox was twenty-five years old, barely older than most of you," Ben added, pretending to be speaking to a room full of undergraduates and becoming comfortable with the role play. "What he accomplished saved the city of Boston from the redcoats and demonstrated the ingenuity of the American soldier."

The inexperienced teacher went on to explain, with intoxicating enthusiasm and detail, how Henry Knox moved fifty-nine pieces of artillery from recently captured Fort Ticonderoga and Crown Point in Upstate New York, near Lake Champlain, in the middle of winter, over trails, frozen lakes, and untamed forest to Boston. The guns were placed at Dorchester Heights, and used to force the British to evacuate the city, which they had occupied since their victory in the Battle of Bunker Hill nine months earlier.

"Plenty of reason to be excited about visiting the historical marker right?"

The professors looked at each other, smiling and nodding. The men were clearly impressed and enjoyed Ben's lecture.

"That will do, Mr. Gilsum. That will do quite nicely. Now we normally discuss your grading techniques and ask for a demonstration or explanation of your process, but you've never taught before so I'm not going to ask you to do that today," Dr. Orchard said mercifully.

"There's only one more task for you. We need you to give us a writing sample. I'll choose the topic and we'll leave you alone for about ninety minutes to write an essay. We've provided a laptop for you to do some research and then type it out. Dr. Gross and I are going to step out for a bit and we'll be back in an hour and a half to wrap up your interview. Your topic is one I'm sure you'll appreciate. Tell me about Dr. Joseph Warren, the influential founding father, lost at the Battle of Bunker Hill," Dr. Orchard said with a smile to his favorite student.

Ben couldn't help but wonder if his friend had purposefully lobbed him a softball to hit out of the park. *I'm going to ace this one.*

Ben had written a thesis paper about Dr. Joseph Warren his senior year in Dr. Orchard's Early American History Class. The two had spent hours discussing the paper, in which Ben described the influence of the fallen hero in the early days of the American Revolution. Ben knew more about Dr. Joseph Warren than most of the authors of any articles he would find on the web using the laptop his interviewers provided him. He wrote his essay, without pause, in thirty minutes and spent the next hour proofreading and perfecting his words.

Dr. Orchard returned alone. "Dr. Gross had to leave us, but he wanted me to tell you he's very impressed with your interview and looks forward to reading your essay. I've no doubt he'll be pleased with it," the professor added with a smile.

"Ben, I want to tell you why I kept interrupting you while you were telling us how grateful you were to be invited here. We both know how terrible you are at accepting compliments, and how uncomfortable you are when they're given. I know you, and I know what you're capable of. I also know your impoverished upbringing left you with some subconscious idea that you're not good enough. It's nonsense. Dr. Gross doesn't know you and I didn't want him to see you expressing any doubt, so I stopped you before you showed any. You deserve to be here, and you proved it today."

Ben nodded. He was clearly uncomfortable and unsure how to respond, but he maintained eye contact with the old professor.

"Aside from your stellar coursework here at John Brown, there was something else that worked in your favor and persuaded Dr. Gross to allow me to bring you in for an interview. I reached out to your former boss, Chuck Woodmere, for a recommendation."

Ben immediately felt horrified. *Oh, shit. No way that went well.*

The young man remembered the look on Chuck's face, back in DC, when he surprised him with a two week notice. A notice that Chuck denied before he instructed security to immediately escort Ben out of the building. The company never allowed employees to serve any notice, due to security concerns. This scene played out on the day he was supposed to start a new position that Chuck had just promoted him to.

"Don't look so scared, Mr. Gilsum," Dr. Orchard laughed. "I remembered Chuck from when the company began recruiting you. He and I had several conversations about you three years ago. It was my turn to ask *him* about *you*. He wrote a beautiful letter on your behalf to the university. He explained how your thirst for knowledge and truth along with your unwavering sense of morality made you an outstanding analyst at the company. Those qualities would certainly serve you well at a Christian university."

Chapter 5
Summer of 2011 – Raymond, Maine

Robert Rindge drove his wife and thirteen-year old twins two and a half hours north on Interstate 95 to Raymond, Maine, where they planned to spend the next ten days in their newly purchased lake house. The Sebago Lake waterfront home sat on the west side of a two by four mile section of the lake, known as Jordan Bay. Though it was a four season home, it would serve as a vacation house for the Rindge family. Robert, the only member of the family to see the house, could hardly contain his excitement. He enjoyed visions of swimming, fishing, and boating with his wife and children as he drove them to the beautiful lake house in Maine.

"Is this our lake house?" an excited Alex Rindge shouted as they finally pulled into the driveway.

"That's the one, kids," their proud father answered, feeling the family's approval and savoring it.

"Mom, look at the lake. It's incredible," Angelina added, getting out of the car and running up to the front door with Alex right behind her.

"Robert, this is beautiful," Deanne Rindge said to her husband as they followed slowly behind, holding hands.

"It's so quiet and peaceful. I expected to see people out on the water," Deanne added.

"It'll pick up this weekend. It's Wednesday. We'll have the bay to ourselves until Saturday," Robert said proudly.

The modest 1800 square-foot home quickly won them over with its stunning scenery and perfect landscaping. One side of the property faced Jordan Bay, with a manicured beach at the water, and the other side bordered a small canal with a dock for safe and easy boat entry to the lake. The entire property was surrounded by beautifully placed short-stone walls, even along the water, with an opening at the beach.

The children picked their bedrooms and the family unpacked the new Land Rover that Mr. Rindge had purchased specifically for winter trips to the family's new camp, which happened to be a half hour drive from three ski resorts.

As the sun sank low in the evening sky, it was time for dinner and discussion about plans to get out on the water the next day. Robert had a huge surprise planned for them. A brand new twenty-foot fiberglass speed-boat would be delivered first thing in the morning. The Rindge family settled down for dinner in a gazebo close to their private beach.

"Dad, look at that boat. Why is it on the grass?" a curious Alex asked.

"I don't know, Son. It probably doesn't even float. Look at the thing. It's pretty beat up and old. Someone must have thought that crazy old rowboat made a nice lawn decoration or something. Maybe they were gonna use it as a giant flower pot," Robert laughed, trying without success to get his kids to laugh with him.

"I bet it floats. Can we try? We can drag it right into the water from there," Alex continued, pointing to the beach.

"I'll tell you what. After dinner we'll go inside and talk about what there is to do around here and make plans for tomorrow. I promise you one thing, Buddy. By lunch time tomorrow, you'll have no interest in that old rowboat. You won't even know it's there."

After dinner, the family decided to spend the entire next day at the new house, swimming and maybe even fishing down by the beach or off the dock in the canal. Robert nearly gave away his secret about the new boat three times, but managed to keep it from the children and his wife.

"Honey, can you come with me? We need to head into town for fishing supplies. We don't even have poles, but we can get everything we need and be back here in plenty of time for bed. Kids, you stay out of the water while Mom and I head to town, OK?'

"Oh, I don't know if we should leave them alone," Deanne protested.

"They'll be fine, dear. They're thirteen years old."

"I need to talk to you about something," Robert said with a whisper, deciding it would be best to give his wife a heads up about the boat being delivered in the morning.

"OK, fine. But let's get back before dark. Kids, I don't want you in that water while we're gone. Is that understood?" Mrs. Rindge said to her children.

"Understood, Mom," both kids answered.

Alex watched his parents pull out of the driveway and drive out of sight. "Angel, let's see if that boat floats."

"Are you deaf? *Both* Mom and Dad said to stay out of the water. We can't"

"Duh. What do you think a boat's for? We won't be in the water, we'll be on that boat," Alex answered with a proud smile.

Angelina smiled back, mischievously. "You're still an idiot, but that's a good point."

The twins made their way down to the old rowboat and were able to drag it across the beach with little effort. Much to Alex's delight, it appeared seaworthy. "I knew it would float," Alex said with glee.

"OK, punk, it floats. Now let's get this thing back up on the grass, before Mom and Dad get home and see us out here."

Alex had other plans. "No way, not yet. Let's take it out. Come on, Angel. Just a quick trip around that side and back?" Alex pleaded, pointing to the canal on the other side of the house.

Angelina took a deep breath and closed her eyes. She wanted to say no, but her brother was never this adventurous. She'd always been the courageous one. She enjoyed seeing him so excited to do something that didn't involve his computer, or a book. "Fine, Alex. Just over there and back," she agreed.

Alex jumped in first while Angelina held the boat steady and then she joined her brother. Each child worked an oar like a paddle on a canoe, neither bothering to place the pinned oars into their proper locations on the boat with the oarlock horns.

The children intended to paddle their way to the mouth of the canal, but the relentless, New England wind blew them in the opposite direction, away from the shore.

"Paddle, Alex! We're going the wrong way!"

"It's not working!" Alex yelled back, fumbling with the oar.

Angelina quickly began to realize they weren't going to be able to paddle their way to shore. They were already fifty feet out and drifting faster, but that wasn't their biggest problem.

"The boat has a leak!" Alex said with a shriek.

"Paddle harder!" Angelina cried, pointing out how far they'd been blown from the house.

The children were paddling as hard as they could, but still moving away from their house, now more than a hundred feet away, while the old rowboat slowly filled with water.

"We're too far out. We don't even have life jackets!" Alex shouted, beginning to cry.

"Help us!" Angelina shouted toward the shore, but no one appeared in sight, nor were there any other boats out on the water on a Wednesday afternoon.

With the old leaky rowboat about to sink from beneath them, and their new house getting farther and farther away, Angelina looked at her brother and declared, "Alex, we're gonna have to swim for it. Right now!"

Alex shook his head, crying. "I can't swim that far," he admitted.

"I'll help you. Let's go." Angelina demanded, pulling her panicking brother into the water.

Finally getting her brother away from the sinking rowboat, Angelina convinced him to settle down and doggie paddle.

"Hold onto my shoulder and I'll pull you to shore," Angelina declared.

Angelina Rindge swam as hard and steady as she could, not looking where she was going. Alex did his best to hold on and kick his feet to push his sister along. After ten minutes, Angelina stopped and needed to rest, but Alex still held firmly onto her shoulder, making it hard for her to tread water. They were still about fifty feet from the shore.

"Alex, doggie paddle for a minute. I need a break"

"I can't," Alex cried, panicking and dipping under water, coughing.

Angelina gave up on having a rest and grabbed her brother with one hand, stroking the water with the other, determined to drag him to shore. In the confusion, she didn't realize they were now swimming in the wrong direction.

Angelina Rindge felt exhausted. She couldn't hold herself and her brother above water any longer. She stopped swimming and tried to calm Alex, but as soon as she did he tried to climb on top of her, pushing her head under water. She fought as long as she could, but had to swim away. She stopped and turned, but couldn't find Alex. She could no longer hear him splashing or yelling or coughing.

"Alex! Where are you?" Angelina cried out.

She swam back to where she believed she'd held on to him before, but couldn't find him above or below the water. She screamed his name over and over, but no one answered. Angelina sobbed uncontrollably, feeling helpless. She looked through tear-filled eyes and saw how far she'd drifted from the shore. She knew she would have to go now, or she would never make it.

The Rindge family sold their lake house in Maine, along with the Land Rover and new speed boat they never used. Robert Rindge hired an overqualified child psychologist from Poland named Marta to be the family's domestic helper. Her duties included rebuilding the Rindge's devastated, heart-broken daughter. Marta would become Angelina's nanny, tutor, and best friend. She would also ensure the Rindge's only surviving child would never be left alone until she became an adult.

Chapter 6

A slow afternoon at work was typical for Ben Gilsum, who always attacked his assignments first thing in the morning, without pause, and completed everything required for the day by lunchtime. The newly-named cost estimator at the plant, who recently returned home to Decatur, Arkansas from adventures untold in the nation's capital, sat at his desk, staring at a ring on his right hand. The large, plain-gold ring, with the letter M engraved on the bezel, once belonged to Bradford Sullivan, and it still gave Ben the creeps every time he looked at it.

Ben had become a member of a secret society during his time in DC called the Brothers of Herrad, which was founded by a former Freemason about fifty years prior. Jim Tamworth, the founding member, known to Ben as Mr. James, quickly became a mentor and close friend. The ring on Ben's finger had been passed from Mr. James to Bradford Sullivan and then to Ben Gilsum, through Mr. James' grandson, Doug Tamworth, a lawyer in Kansas City who handled his grandfather's communication. It was worn by the leader, or Worshipful Master, of the Brothers of Herrad.

Ben rose quickly to Worshipful Master because the now ninety-nine year old Mr. James saw the young man's incredible potential. The quick ascension was also due to the fact that Ben, an Intelligence Analyst at the time, exposed Bradford Sullivan and his son Billy as criminals who were using their affiliation with the Brothers to launder money generated by their illegal activity in the form of donations to the secret society. Some of the money went to the organization, but much more went into the Sullivans' pockets. Mr. James, a very wealthy man, also rewarded Ben with the old church building he intended to use to start The Decatur Club for Boys and Girls and a handsome donation to cover operating expenses. A dream come true for Ben.

How am I supposed to be Worshipful Master when every single time I look at this ring I think about Washington, DC and get creeped out? Why did I accept the position? Why did I promise to start a new lodge at the old church? I haven't even begun to look for new members. Maybe I should call Doug Tamworth and tell him I don't want to be…

A vibrating cell phone in the less than enthusiastic Worshipful Master's pocket pulled him away from his thoughts. *John Brown University?*

"Hello, this is Ben."

"Mr. Gilsum, it's Dr. Orchard from John Brown. I hope you're having a good day, young man. I believe I'm about to make it even better."

Ben's heart pounded as he began to realize what his former history professor and current head of the history department at John Brown University, was about to tell him.

"We've decided to offer you a position here at JBU. Not the Associate Professor position you applied for, to be clear. As we discussed during your interview, we're offering you the position of Assistant Professor."

"Dr. Orchard, I'm nearly too excited to speak. You can't imagine what this means to me. Thank you so much."

"I believe I can. And you're the right person for the job. I've spent the last ten days convincing Dean Gross of that, my friend. I know you'll prove me right."

Emotion started to get the best of the young man, but he contained himself as his future boss explained the details of an offer letter, which would be emailed accordingly after the two men finished their conversation.

"I want to be clear that the Assistant Professor title is the first step of a tenured professorship. It's almost always given to someone with a doctoral degree. This is quite an honor, particularly at a fine university like John Brown."

"I understand, Dr. Orchard. I'm thrilled to be given this opportunity. I've already made plans to complete my education and catch up with the rest of the faculty in that regard. I won't let you down."

"There's one more thing you'll need to work on immediately," Dr. Orchard added. "We need to get you published. Quickly."

"Published? I've never done any writing. I'm not sure how to begin being published."

"Mr. Gilsum, don't let this make you nervous. I've helped several young professors make this happen, none of them as gifted as you. The writing sample you submitted during the interview process about Dr. Joseph Warren is practically magazine worthy as it stands. I'll work with you to beef that up to say, twelve thousand words? And then we'll submit it to some American history journals who will be honored to publish it. After that, you'll make it a book."

"Book? You think I'm ready for a book?" Ben asked, questioning if he'd made the right decision.

"Oh yes, Mr. Gilsum. You're going to be a college professor, and an author, before I'm done with you. The concepts in your paper are exciting stuff. And you backed up those concepts with more than just fiery emotion. You convinced me of ideas about Dr. Joseph Warren I'd never even considered. You, sir, are a natural. I'll help you believe that."

Ben wasn't about to reply to the compliment. He hated compliments and Dr. Orchard knew it.

"Don't worry, young man. I'm not going to wait on the line for you to accept the kind words. Read the offer letter carefully. Take some time to consider it. When you realize what I already know—this is the opportunity of a lifetime, and one you were born for—sign the offer letter and return it to me. We have plenty of time to discuss the rest."

Chapter 7
Summer of 2017 - Wellesley, Massachusetts

"With twenty-three seconds on the clock, freshman sensation, point guard Emily Cantwell moves the ball past center court for Dartmouth. The Big Green, down just one point, can run the clock out and take the game winner against Harvard."

"Samantha, how sweet would it be to knock off the division leader here, and finish the season with a winning record? I'm guessing fourteen and thirteen has a nice ring to it for the Big Green."

"Absolutely, Jim. These women made a late season surge on the backs of Cantwell and senior forward Angel Rindge, who is very likely playing her last competitive basketball game. Only the top four teams in the division play in the division championship tournament. I wouldn't be surprised to see Cantwell find Rindge underneath for the game winner in the next ten seconds."

"There she goes. Rindge into the paint looking to create a passing lane for Cantwell. Cantwell finds Rindge underneath. And she's done it! Senior forward Angel Rindge just blew past the defender for an easy layup, right at the buzzer. That's the season folks. And that's the end of Hanover favorite, Angelina Rindge's basketball career here at Dartmouth. Thanks for the memories, Angel. We're sure gonna miss you."

Angelina Rindge lay on top of her bed, dressed and ready to go. The young woman waited for her ride, while daydreaming about her last basketball game at Dartmouth College.

In the six months after that memorable moment, she graduated with honors and a degree in government, got accepted to law school, and received a job offer in Washington, DC as a personal assistant to the junior senator of Massachusetts, who happened to be a close friend of her father. Angelina prepared to catch a flight from Boston to the nation's capital to start her job, and attend law school.

"Are you ready to go, my lovely?" Marta asked with a thick Polish accent from the doorway of Angelina's bedroom, after spending a moment in silence staring at her beloved Angelina.

The domestic helper, hired to take care of Angelina after her twin brother died, stood barely five feet tall. She had short, light-brown hair and a round face with big, friendly blue eyes. She'd become a best friend to Angelina, and had done an excellent job rebuilding the shattered young girl who watched her brother drown at the age of thirteen. Angelina acquired much of Marta's spunk to compliment her already spirited nature.

Angelina grew into a tall, slender, and strikingly beautiful young woman. Her long brown hair, bright blue eyes, and brilliant smile garnered plenty of attention, but her outgoing and cheerful personality made her irresistible to most people. She was full of life and loved adventure.

"Can't you come with me, Marta? We could be roommates. You don't need to stick around here anymore. I'm all grown up."

"You may be grown, but you're still a spoiled brat, my Angel. That much is true," the short, rotund Marta answered with a smile. "But no, I don't wanna go to Washington, DC and live with a twenty-one-year-old. I'm an old woman. What use would you have for me there? I will stay here and keep an eye on your mom and dad. They need me more than you."

"Blah," Angelina answered, more excited than nervous about being alone in a new city.

"What about Mr. Billy Sullivan? He's there, isn't he? Your hot boyfriend from last year? Maybe you rekindle an old flame?"

Angelina pretended to throw up and answered, "Never. That douchebag? Are you kidding me, Marta?"

"Please don't speak like that to me. What's so bad about Billy? I thought he was cute. And he asked you to marry him when he found out you were coming to Washington, right? He's sure ready to light that flame."

Angelina laughed, a little too loudly, and answered, "Oh yeah, *the proposal of a lifetime.* All he's after, now that he's out there with his father, doing God knows what for the government, is a connection to Daddy and his political friends. Those two have been after my father and his money for years. If I told Daddy that Billy asked me to marry him, he'd make me cancel my flight immediately and find a law school in New England. He's nervous enough about me being in DC alone. He's been lecturing me for days. Billy and I are over. O-V-A-H, ovah. I'm sure we'll see each other in DC, but there won't be any lighting of any old flames, my dear Marta. No chance."

The two were headed to Logan Airport in Marta's minivan, after a long and tearful goodbye with Deanne Rindge. Robert Rindge kept his goodbye short and sweet. He told his daughter how proud she made him feel, and repeated himself, for what Angelina counted as the one-hundredth time, telling her to be careful who she spent time with. No one in Washington, DC was to be trusted.

"Why are you so quiet, lovely? This is not like you," Marta asked, concerned.

"I think I might actually be nervous. I'm even starting to feel a little nauseous about the whole thing."

"Nauseous? Don't you be sick in my car. You tell me if you're about to throw up and I pull over, OK?"

Angelina laughed. "Don't worry, Marta. I'm not gonna boot in the minivan."

"That's good. You remember your basketball trip to Timothy Peak? The one where everyone got sick?" Marta asked, changing the subject.

"Ugh. Why would you bring that up? That was norovirus, not nerves, and I've tried to erase the entire weekend from my memory."

"You start talking about puking and that's the first thing I think of. You brought it up, not me."

"I was eleven years old, playing travel basketball. We had fifteen players and forty-five parents and siblings for the weekend at Timothy Peak Resort, which was actually an awesome place, in Vermont. On the last night of the tournament, all the parents went out for dinner, leaving most of the kids and siblings to one townhouse with an older sister in charge. I still feel sorry for her, she was a sweetheart, too. What a night," Angelina recalled.

"I was the first one to throw up, and we called my parents. They were convinced that I had just eaten too much junk food and all the running around had made me sick. Then on their way to come and get me, another kid booted, then another, and then another. By the end of the weekend, fifty-seven of our group of sixty experienced the hell of norovirus, and we had to cancel the championship game on Sunday. Did you know that poor girl, left in charge of us maniacs, never even got sick? After all the carnage? She should have been the one taking home a trophy from that nightmare," Angelina declared.

"I just love that story," Marta said with a laugh.

"Well, I sure don't, but thank you for bringing it up anyway. I think I actually feel better now. Nothing will ever be that bad. I hope."

"That's my girl. That's been my plan all along. You're going to be just fine out there, my Angel. There's nothing Angelina Rindge can't handle. Nothing."

Chapter 8

The soon-to-be Assistant Professor at John Brown University drove his Jeep Wrangler on East Roller Ave, out of Decatur, past the churches and chicken farms, where East Roller becomes Highway 102. He was on his way to pick up Patty at the Northwest Arkansas Regional Airport in Bentonville. The young couple hadn't seen each other for months.

Ben's mind wandered during the drive, trying to figure out how he would reply to Dr. Orchard's email that contained the offer letter. He'd already signed and scanned the letter, but hadn't sent it back yet. In typical Ben Gilsum, stress-over-every-detail fashion, he agonized about what he would say in his return email.

Ben began talking to himself. "He already told me he didn't want me to be overly thankful. Said it showed a lack of confidence, or something like that. But I am overly thankful. And I want him to know it."

"I don't know, maybe I'll just keep it short and sweet. 'Thank you for the opportunity. I accept your offer. Can't wait to get started. Your pal, Ben Gilsum.' Or should I demand more money?" Ben laughed at himself and quickly changed his topic of thought to Patty.

The young couple would enjoy Patty's first night in Arkansas, Friday evening, alone in Bentonville, before heading to Decatur for dinner on Saturday at the Gilsum's home. Patty would then fly back to DC on Sunday. Ben tried to suggest they all go *out* to dinner, attempting to keep Patty away from the house as much as possible. His mother would have none of that. She was already bothered, as was Mr. Gilsum, over the fact that Ben's guest would only be in Decatur for one day. The fact that she would be staying at a hotel, out of town, didn't help either.

Mrs. Gilsum's complaints echoed in Ben's mind. "Baby, why does she have to hide over in Bentonville, away from us? Why can't she stay here? How are we going to get to know her? Something just isn't right about any of this."

Mrs. Gilsum's health was failing. Diagnosed with muscular dystrophy soon after Ben's birth, her condition caused her to be in and out of work. By the time her son entered junior high school, she had regressed and could no longer work. More recently, things had been getting rapidly worse, but she was excited to meet Ben's friend from Washington, DC and determined to spend time with her. She had hoped Angelina Rindge would be the one Ben brought home from the nation's capital, and she wasn't afraid to tell her son that, repeatedly.

Mrs. Gilsum had a habit of finding faults in most girls her only son dated, and she had already found plenty in Patty. But Ben's

Angel, Angelina, was perfect in her mind. This Patty was clearly a distraction that had to be suffered until her son came to his senses and won Angel's heart back. She had no idea why Ben broke it off with Angelina, nor did she care. Angel made Ben better, and Angel was the one for her son.

Ben waited at the security entrance of Concourse A for Patty. *Why am I not more excited about this? Too much on my mind probably with JBU and the new job. I better snap out of it before she gets here.*

"Excuse me, Sir. Do you know where I can find the sexiest man alive? He's being held captive, far away from me, in the beautiful state of *Are-Kansas,"* Patty declared playfully, getting Ben's attention, pulling him from his daydream. "Oh wait, he's you."

When Ben came to his senses she wrapped him in a warm hug and gave him a long kiss. The beautiful, petite redhead with green eyes and bright smile quickly brought Ben to attention. *This is going to be a great weekend.*

"Sorry about that, I was spacing out. You look amazing. I'm so happy to see you."

"Now that's much more like it, sweetie. And you are a tall, dark, and hella-handsome sight for sore eyes. Now let's blow this popsicle stand so I can show you how happy I am to see you," Patty answered.

Hella?

"So I have a pretty interesting spot in mind for dinner. You remember the Bonefish Grill in Alexandria?" Ben asked on the drive to the hotel.

"Of course I do. It was one of our favorite places. They have one out here in the sticks?"

"You're gonna be a little surprised when you see this place. South Market Street in Rogers is pretty cool. There's a bunch of nice restaurants and bars, it's kinda upscale…"

"Rogers? Is that far? Oh sweetie, doesn't the hotel have room service?"

"It's only a twenty minute drive from the hotel. I made a reservation for…"

"Ben, sweetie," Patty interrupted a second time, placing her hand high on Ben's thigh. "Let's blow off the reservation, get naked, and if you survive what I have planned for you, I'll let you call room service so you can regain your strength. Then we can do it again."

"Oh. Well. You know we can always check out South Market Street some other time," Ben answered with a smile, his stomach growling because he had skipped lunch to leave work early and meet Patty at the airport.

The Wingate Hotel in Bentonville, Arkansas was a four story building two miles from the airport. The hotel was surrounded by big, empty grass fields that were covered in the fall with large, round hay bales, produced for surrounding farms. Ben thought Patty would like the scenery and felt excited to bring her there.

"Holy shit. Look at this place," Patty exclaimed as she climbed out of the Jeep in the hotel parking lot. "We're literally in the middle of nowhere. How can you stand it?"

"They have an indoor pool and hot tub," Ben reminded his out-of-town guest, hoping to sell the place a little more. He tried to hide the fact that he felt annoyed and smiled. "You brought your bathing suit, right?"

"No, Ben. I didn't bring my bikini. And I'm not planning on wasting any time hanging out poolside," Patty answered with a seductive kiss.

Chapter 9

Ben woke early Saturday morning at the Wingate Hotel. Just enough sunlight spilled around the shade over the window to allow him to see the youthful, fair skin of the naked and uncovered Patty lying beside him. *My God, she's beautiful. Wish I knew why I wasn't more excited to see her.*

Ben gazed at Patty with awe. He wondered if he should risk waking her by getting out of bed and making a cup of terrible coffee with the contraption provided near the door, across from the bathroom. *It's way too early.*

The young man turned onto his back and stared at the ceiling instead. *When should we go see my parents? How about never?*

He remembered how excited he'd felt at the idea of his parents meeting Patty. How for the first time in his life he actually wanted to bring someone home. Now he felt confused about what was happening. *I knew I was in love with Patty in Virginia. There wasn't any doubt. All the late nights on the phone after I left? I still felt it. What the hell is happening?*

A terrible thought came to Ben and he quickly dismissed it as impossible, given what happened in Alexandria. *What if I was just lonely? Hurting over Angel? What if I never got over her? Ugh, I need to get over this. Today's gonna be great. Patty's great. My parents will come to their senses and love her like I do. But do I?*

Three hours and a few unsuccessful attempts to wake Patty later, the positively frustrated Ben Gilsum was pulled back to reality and answered the buzzing cell phone on the night stand next to the bed.

"Hi, Mom. Good morning."

"Morning? Oh, is it still morning? I thought it was lunch time already," a clearly unhappy Mrs. Gilsum answered back.

Patty began to stir, next to Ben. She pulled a sheet over her naked body and rolled on her side facing him.

"Who are you talking to? What time is it?" Patty asked in an obviously sleepy voice, before rolling onto her back and covering her face with her pillow.

"Oh, Baby, are you two not even up yet?" Mrs. Gilsum asked. "You know what, I'm gonna hang up the phone now. Please call me when you're up. Your father and I would like to know when you'll be home. We were under the impression we would spending time with you and your friend at some point today," Mrs. Gilsum added before hanging up on her son.

"Oh, God. This is gonna be a hell of a day," Ben declared, tossing his cell phone back onto the night stand, covering his eyes with his palms, letting out a long, conceding exhale.

"Oh, boy. Is Mommy being a pain in the ass?" Patty asked, sliding closer and laying her head on Ben's chest.

"Something like that," Ben answered putting one arm over Patty's shoulder, and the other behind his head. *Just get me through this one day.*

"We do need to get moving. Let me describe the current scene at my house for you. Right now my mother's giving my father an earful, which he's doing his very best to ignore. When that's over she'll call back and give me an earful, which will be worse than what she's giving my father because I won't be able to ignore her."

"What's the rush? I'm only here for one more night," Patty declared, pulling herself up over Ben, kissing him softly.

A buzzing cell phone, on the night stand next to the bed, interrupted the young couple before Ben had an opportunity to respond to Patty's advance. He answered the phone again, much to his beautiful girlfriend's anguish.

"OK, Mom. We're leaving here as soon as possible."

The young couple quickly showered and made their way to Decatur, neither speaking much along the way. Patty sensed Ben's frustration and she felt plenty of her own. She turned up the volume on the radio to a decibel level that rendered conversation impossible and stared out the window for the entire twenty minute drive. Twenty minutes felt like twenty hours to Ben, who enjoyed listening to Taylor Swift about as much as the sound of the drill at the dentist.

You've got to be fucking kidding me.

Chapter 10

Mrs. Gilsum, a tall, full-figured woman with short dark hair, sat on the front porch of the family's home, reading a book, when her son and his guest pulled into the driveway. It was much later than she'd hoped for. She closed her prized copy of *Becoming Michelle Obama* and took a deep breath, then released it with force. She took her oversized, black-brimmed reading glasses off, letting them hang around her neck with a silver eyeglass chain, and greeted her guest. *Here we go.*

"Patty, it's lovely to finally meet you. Oh, your hair is so beautiful. Even if you had no time to style it or anything. It looks just fine like that. Just get up and go. I'm a little jealous," Mrs. Gilsum admitted.

After an awkward pause, Patty started to answer, "Well, we were a bit rushed this morning. But you know…"

"Dad! Where you at old man?" Ben interrupted loudly. "Come meet Patty." *Please God, save me.*

"What's all the yelling about in here?" a confused Mr. Gilsum asked. "Oh. Well, hello there, little lady. You must be Patty. It's very nice to meet you. And you're far too pretty to be wasting your time with the likes of this homely feller over here. Son, you didn't tell me you was datin' a movie star."

"Mr. Gilsum, it's a pleasure to meet you," Patty answered with a blush and smile, relieved to be getting some good vibes. She offered a handshake and Mr. Gilsum pulled her hand to his lips and gave it a peck.

"OK, enough of that, old man. Let the girl breath," Mrs. Gilsum said. "Come on everyone, I have some sweet tea waiting for us outside on the picnic table. We can go out there and get some fresh air, then I'll get started on dinner."

Patty grabbed Ben's hand as the four walked outside to an old picnic table, under a big oak tree in the Gilsum's back yard. The table had existed back there as long as Ben could remember, on a grassless patch of dirt and sand, the legs held together by sheer will alone. Ben noticed the rotting boards with dirt clinging to the bottom and sides of the old table and immediately felt embarrassed by the humble setting. He looked back at their small house, with a sagging roof and a broken half-fence that surrounded the yard. He took a deep breath and looked at Patty who smiled at him, clearly not bothered by the couple's surroundings. He couldn't help but let out a small laugh in relief. *She really is special. Maybe this won't be so bad after all.*

"So Patty, Ben hasn't told me what you do back in Washington," Mrs. Gilsum said, staring the conversation.

Ben gave his mother a confused look. He remembered telling her several times that Patty worked as a waitress at his favorite spot in Alexandria for a drink, the Columbia Firehouse on King Street.

"He hasn't?" Patty answered, giving Ben a sharp look. "I'm a waitress. I'm really surprised he didn't tell you that considering I served him every Thursday in Alexandria." She looked over at Mr. Gilsum, who appeared to be hanging on her every word, staring like a puppy begging for a treat, and continued, "Every Thursday, for two years, I tried to get this guy's attention, hoping he would notice I was sweet on him. Your incredibly handsome son here—he's one tough nut to crack."

"The boy's an idiot," Mr. Gilsum declared bluntly.

Mrs. Gilsum shot her husband a look as Ben erupted into laughter. "You must know his Angel then?" she asked.

Ben stopped laughing immediately upon hearing the question, feeling the tension building in the air. *Oh shit.*

"His Angel? If you mean Angelina from back in Alexandria, yes, I did know her. She's gone back to Boston, and unless there's something you haven't told me, Ben, I don't believe she's *your Angel* anymore," Patty answered.

"So, Mom, what are we having for dinner? You need some help getting that started?" Ben diverted.

"Oh baby, it's still a little early. I'm making a roasted chicken and mashed potatoes. And after, we'll have peach cobbler."

Mrs. Gilsum, the former elementary school teacher, was famous in Decatur for her peach cobbler. Though she'd had to give up teaching years earlier for health reasons, she remained involved in school fund raisers and bake sales. She was a much-loved member of the town.

"Are you trying to change the subject, sweetie? Cause I'd love to talk more about *your Angel,"* Patty persisted.

"Run, idiot, run!" Mr. Gilsum advised his son with a belly laugh.

Ben became irritated with Patty again, and the obvious tension between her and his mother wasn't helping. "There's really nothing to talk about. You summed it up perfectly. She's *completely* out of the picture," Ben declared.

The frustrated young man looked directly at his mother. "She's not my anything. She's back in Boston for good. Story over."

"Well, a mother sometimes knows more about these things than her children," Mrs. Gilsum concluded. She took a look at Patty and added, "Knows more than other children, too."

Mr. Gilsum finally picked up on the obvious tension, "Ladies, if you'll excuse me, the Cardinals are on. I think it's time I go check the score. I'll be back in a second," he added, though everyone, except Patty, knew that meant he'd be gone until dinner.

Ben and his father shared a passion for baseball, and they typically tried their best to watch all one hundred and sixty two Cardinal games every season. This game, however, didn't have much appeal for Ben. *Nice excuse, Dad. It's the last series of the season, and they're in fourth place. This game is meaningless. Actually, kinda wish I could join you right about now.*

Patty, never one to back down from a fight, knew she couldn't win this contest. She surrendered, saying nothing more about Angelina, or anything else for that matter. She'd been jealous of Angelina Rindge for as long as she'd known her. The beautiful girl from Boston came out of nowhere in Alexandria, and swept Ben away from her. Angelina accomplished in days what Patty had failed for two years to do—break through Ben's shell. Even after Ben promised things were over between him and Angelina, Patty remained insecure. *And now his mother loves her, too.*

The foursome shared an increasingly uncomfortable and quiet dinner together. Ben tried to make eye contact and smile at Patty several times. The young woman looked away. He knew he should take her away or, at the very least, for a walk outside to try and reassure her, but he wasn't even sure he wanted to. This long-anticipated visit had quickly spiraled out of control, worse than the worrisome Ben Gilsum could have imagined.

The ride back to the hotel started out in silence, until Ben finally spoke. "Patty, I'm really sorry about all of that. I have no idea what got into my mother. She's been tough on my girlfriends before, but that was ridiculous. You didn't deserve that."

"Why bother? She obviously hates me. I would say I don't know why, but that's pretty obvious, too," Patty said, coldly. "I refuse to compete with Angelina Rindge. Not for you, and not for your mother, either. I give up."

"It's not like that. I don't even…"

"Don't bother, Ben," Patty interrupted, crying.

"I'm gonna head back home tonight and set things straight. I'll come back to the hotel in the morning. We can hang out a while until it's time to head to the airport…"

"Wow! Really? Don't bother coming at all, Ben. I'll catch an Uber to the airport."

As the couple pulled into the hotel parking lot, Patty let herself out of the Jeep. Before she slammed the door and walked into the hotel she said one last thing to Ben Gilsum.

"Tough nut to crack."

Chapter 11

Fall of 2018 – Washington, D.C.

Billy Sullivan sat in his dark-blue Mercedes S-Class Sedan just outside the Columbia Firehouse off of King Street. The beautifully restored building, originally constructed around 1870 and home to the Columbia Steam Engine Fire Company, was now a popular restaurant and bar in Old Town, the historic center of Alexandria, Virginia.

King Street was a favorite spot for tourists. A popular landmark, the George Washington Masonic National Memorial rested at its beginning, near a Metro stop on the top of a hill that sloped downward to the Potomac River. There were museums, popular coffee shops, restaurants and bars along the way, and on the waterfront at the bottom of the hill.

The attractive young man, with his dark hair slicked back, watched Ben Gilsum walk into the Columbia Firehouse. He pulled his cell phone out of his coat pocket and called his father, Bradford Sullivan.

"Yeah, Dad. He's here. Every fucking Thursday. Same time. This guy really needs to get a life."

"Excellent work, Son. This is going to be too easy. And William, you shouldn't swear so much. You sound unprofessional. Like an amateur."

Billy ignored his father's criticism and asked, "You sure this guy's got the nerve to be who we need him to be? He doesn't look like much to me."

"He actually couldn't be more perfect if we'd designed him ourselves. When Ted Seneca retires, Ben Gilsum is a lock to take over his position at the company. That alone makes him our first choice."

"But will he be able to handle the pressure? Ted has balls to spare. He's tough, a former hockey player. He's fearless. I hate to tell ya, Dad, this guy seems soft to me."

Bradford took a minute to consider what his son had said. "Let me paint you a picture of Ben Gilsum, and explain how this is going to work. He spends every Saturday at the Boys and Girls Club in town, volunteering to coach local underprivileged kids. Raising thousands, perhaps millions, of dollars for children's charities will appeal to him immediately. On top of that, he's a history fanatic. Another reason the Brothers will appeal to him. My associates at the government, and the company, are convinced he's an empath. They spent a great deal of effort searching for someone just like him to recruit for his position at the company."

Billy hesitated, then let out a chuckle, still not impressed.

Bradford continued, "Wait until I tell the old man, Mr. James, about this guy. I can see him drooling already. The two practically share the same personality. The Brothers are going to want him as much as he's going to want the Brothers. And then there's my favorite part. He grew up poor. Really poor. If it comes to it, we can offer him a lifestyle he's never imagined. But that may not even be necessary. That's just my backup plan."

"Well, shit, Dad. Backup plan? Why not just use the money as Plan A? Money like that should be enough to win anyone over. Shouldn't it? It's easy, and I always prefer easy over hard. Money should definitely appeal to a poor, dumb hick like this guy," Billy added, concerned about the complexity of the plan.

Bradford laughed. "Not a man like Ben Gilsum. And he may be a poor hick, but he's far from dumb. We have all the things we need to win him over. He'll take far less convincing than Ted did. And cost less. The only thing we're missing is someone close to him to keep him happy. Encourage him a little, distract him for a while. Let us know if he's getting spooked. Now are you sure your ex-girlfriend, Miss Angelina Rindge, can handle that?"

Billy gave a short, almost forced laugh, spitting on his windshield. "Oh, she can handle it, Dad. She's a hell of a distraction, too. This little worm from Arkansas won't know what hit him."

"How about you? You two were pretty close. Are you OK with letting her do this?"

Another exaggerated laugh from Billy. "I don't give a shit about her anymore. Let him have her."

Chapter 12

Fall of 2018 – Washington, D.C.

Angelina Rindge sat directly across from the formally dressed and handsome Billy Sullivan. The elegant young woman wore a short black high-necked and form-fitting dinner dress. The two had arranged to meet for dinner and drinks at Fila, a high-end Italian restaurant on Pennsylvania Avenue in Washington, DC. Billy convinced her to meet with him because he had something important to talk with her about. She made him promise, three times, that this was not a date, he wouldn't make a pass at her, and the two would leave separately, heading away in different directions.

"Angel, you look stunning. I can't even see the little tomboy from Wellesley anymore when I look at you. She's gone forever," Billy said, starting the conversation with a compliment for his lovely dinner companion.

"Shut it, Sullivan. You promised," Angelina fired back.

"I know, and I intend to keep that promise. A friend can tell another friend how beautiful she is. Can't he?"

"Well, thank you. Living out here, away from Southie, suits you. You clean up nice."

Billy raised his glass. "Here's to a couple kids from two different sides of the tracks in Boston, living it up like rock stars in Washington. Who knew, right?"

"So, what's this all about? Why do you need my help?" Angelina asked, not ready to trust Billy, or his father.

"Right to business? Fair enough. My father is the one who needs you. I just enjoy your company. I told him I'd meet with you and fill you in on some of the details. You know my dad works for the federal government, in law enforcement, right? Did you know he knows your boss?"

"That's a laugh and a half. We both know your dad is suspect. But yes, I know he works for the government. And he's connected. I also know he and the Senator are close. I've seen Senator Daniels and Dr. Evil together more than once."

"Dr. Evil? Come on Angel, people change. Anyway, he's definitely close with your boss. And quite a few others in high places by the way. My father's associates and Senator Daniels have a mutual interest in a guy who's kinda new here in DC. They need someone to befriend him. Get close to him, keep tabs on him," Billy added, noticing an unsure look on Angelina's face.

"Why hasn't Senator Daniels said anything to me about this guy? I mean, I'm with him every day that he's in town. Why would he ask you two clowns to get involved?"

Billy laughed. "I don't think you realize something. My father and I are completely legit out here. We're not in Boston anymore. We work with some of the most powerful people in the world.

And this type of conversation isn't exactly one a Senator should be having with a personal assistant."

"OK, fine. I thought there was something weird about this. Now I know there is."

"My father will send you all the details you need about the guy. What he's into, where you can find him, how to become friendly with him. It's easy money. And it's a lot of money. Just read the details when you get them. This is important, and a lot less boring than running around town, collecting dry cleaning for the junior Senator from the State of Massachusetts," Billy said, before finishing his glass of red wine.

Angelina managed to escape her encounter with Billy unharmed. *He actually behaved like a gentleman, for once. Maybe this is legit.*

She received the email from Bradford Sullivan the next morning. At first she felt inclined to track him down and punch him in the face for what he suggested she do. "Get close to him. Make him happy. Keep him happy." *Does he think I'm a prostitute?*

And then she thought about the rest of the email. "You can take it as far as you want to, completely your call. Just make sure he likes you, and confides in you. We only need you to keep tabs on him for a while, and tell us if he's unhappy or nervous. When we have what we need, you can end your involvement with him in any way you see fit. Encourage him to join the Brothers of Herrad. That's critical." *Who the hell are the Brothers of Herrad?*

She took the "assignment" and met Ben Gilsum, for the first time, at exactly the place and time the Sullivans suggested. She managed to begin a friendship with him and he behaved exactly as they said he would. But after a short period of time, something happened that neither she nor the Sullivans expected. Angelina Rindge fell in love.

Though Ben behaved just as Bradford said he would, no one prepared Angelina for how wonderful a person the shy-awkward young man from Arkansas really was. Nor did they explain how resourceful he could be. When he discovered what Angelina and everyone else was up to, the fallout ended the careers of all of those involved, including Ben himself. There was one exception; the junior Senator of the State of Massachusetts, who knew nothing of the whole ordeal. Angelina Rindge was left with a deeply broken heart for the second time in her very young life.

Chapter 13

Summer of 2019 – Wellesley, Massachusetts

When Angelina returned to Wellesley, Massachusetts after completing just one year of law school in DC, Robert Rindge knew something terrible had happened but didn't press his daughter for answers. She wasn't harmed, and she'd come home safe. But she seemed unusually somber and quiet. Angelina's behavior reminded Robert of the time her twin brother, Alex, died. He waited a few days and then decided it was time to discuss what went wrong.

His only daughter was staring blankly out the window as Robert entered the sunroom. He took a seat next to her. "Angel, I think it's time we discuss why you left Washington. Senator Daniels told me there was nothing work related, and you surprised him with your resignation. What happened out there?"

Angelina always kept her head up and her voice clear and direct when speaking with her father. When she didn't, as a young child, he corrected her immediately. This conversation was unlike most, and neither father nor daughter stuck to protocol.

"Well, Senator Daniels is a crook, and an asshole," Angelina murmured.

"Angel, did he do something? Sweetheart, there is nothing you can't tell me. I need to know, and we'll deal with it together."

"No. Not to me. And I can't tell you what he's done to anyone else, because I don't know. I just know he's a criminal. I know he associates with criminals. I know it for a fact and I didn't want to be around any of it anymore. I was weak, Dad. I was weak and I let you down. I let myself down, again. Just like with Alex, I wasn't strong enough to say no when I knew something was wrong. Because I was excited about it," Angelina added, crying.

"Honey, what happened with Alex was not your fault. You did everything you could to save him. Your strength is the only reason I didn't lose two children that day. No one has ever blamed you for what happened. Don't do this to yourself."

Angelina gathered herself a little, but remained silent.

"We got through that day. And if we can get through a loss like that, we can get through anything," Robert said softly while placing his palm over his daughter's cheek, then wiping a tear with his thumb and tucking her hair behind her ear.

Angelina stopped crying and looked her father in the eye. She gathered her strength and spoke the way Robert had become accustomed to hearing her speak.

"I have a new plan for what I want to do with the rest of my life. I'm going to finish law school, but I'm getting into law enforcement. I'm going to put criminals, like the ones I know in

DC, in jail. I'm going to start by busting Billy and Bradford Sullivan. Those assholes don't deserve to breathe free air…"

Robert interrupted, "Was it Billy Sullivan who hurt you? I knew it. I knew the Sullivans were in Washington, and I still sent you out there. I'm gonna…"

"Daddy, stop. Look at me. No one hurt me. I'm fine. I don't want you to get involved. I've got this."

Angelina asked her father a question, to change the subject, "Daddy, why do you give money to people like Senator Daniels, or any politician?"

Robert stopped his rant about the Sullivans and changed to a softer tone, indulging his daughter's quick subject change, "They're not all bad. Sometimes the good ones do a great deal of good, for all of us. I was wrong about Daniels. Our association is over, right now."

Robert hugged his daughter and continued, "People like me make donations to politicians for all sorts of reasons. Influence being the most common, I'm afraid. But sometimes we see hope, and we chase after it. Sometimes we're wrong. Power corrupts. I don't want you to tell me any more details about what happened in DC. Unless you want to, of course. You've got this. I'm sure of that, and I'm sure that whatever went wrong out there will make you even stronger. I'm proud of you for making the decision to fight. Those *assholes* have no idea who they're up against."

Chapter 14

The old church building, now Ben's home, sat on four cleared acres of land on the north side of Decatur. Final renovations were still underway for most of the building's interior, which would be home to the Decatur Club for Boys and Girls. But the apartment on the first floor needed no further preparation. The exterior looked better than it had in years, everything was ready. Three fields for various sports were clean and neat, and a newly created basketball court was ready for action.

The four large, stained-glass windows on each side of the second floor were preserved, and Ben had no intention of replacing them. The building was a plain, rectangle-shaped construction with a steeple built into the roof on one side. The cross had been removed some time ago.

The first-floor door opened into a large open area that Ben filled with tables and chairs for art and music lessons, reading, snack time and other activities. The other half of the first floor was closed off with a door to Ben's apartment.

The second floor was split into two sections. The section closest to the second-floor door became a playroom, complete with foosball, ping-pong, and pool tables. The rest of the second floor would serve two purposes—first as an auditorium of sorts for the club and second as home to the Brothers of Herrad lodge Ben had promised to start in Decatur.

The lodge was open, with seating on both sides and a stage at the front of the room. Ben, the Worshipful Master, and other officers would be seated on the stage during the group's monthly assemblies, which were to occur on the first Wednesday of every month. Ben's enthusiasm for moving into his apartment and starting the club far outweighed his motivation for the lodge. Becoming the youngest Assistant Professor at John Brown would eventually consume more time than all of the other activities.

The building sat alone, at least a half mile away from the nearest house or business. With only one outside light on the steeple side, navigating his way to the entrance after dark proved challenging. Ben planned to add another light above the first-floor entrance eventually.

The solitude and setting around the old church reminded Ben of his small apartment in the woods near Mount Vernon in Virginia. He felt at ease in the woods. The time away from others allowed the young man to relax, and gave him the sense of recharging his batteries.

Sometimes, like tonight, it felt lonely, even creepy, considering three quarters of the building remained empty. Ben tried not to think about that as he sat at his desk and Googled Dr. Joseph Warren on his computer.

I'll get used to this place. There's no way I'd be able to focus on work in my tiny bedroom at Mom and Dad's house. This is a HUGE improvement. Besides, that room's been taken.

Mrs. Gilsum's sister, a widow named Lilian, had taken up residence in Ben's room at the Gilsum's home in Decatur. Lilian's husband Victor was killed by a bull in Springdale when Ben was too young to remember. Aunt Lilian and her husband enjoyed going to the rodeo in Springdale every year, and living it up like college kids on spring break.

One year, long after the show was over, a very drunk Victor declared to a very drunk Lilian, and anyone else who would listen, "I'm gonna go pay a visit to the meanest bull at this here rodeo. Red Goliath himself. And I'm gonna piss on that bastard."

Shortly after, the newly widowed Lilian began her metamorphosis, becoming a born again Christian, and slowly changing into the extremely-religious elementary school teacher Ben always remembered her to be.

Aunt Lilian had lived in a small one-room apartment for years after she lost her husband, and never remarried. She was tall, like her sister, but much thinner. She always wore dresses, thick glasses, and kept her curly hair short and neat. Though Lilian taught elementary school, like her sister, she was not beloved by her students. She ran a tight ship, graded strictly, and never tolerated misbehavior of any kind. Especially from the boys in her class.

Aunt Lilian convinced her sister to allow her to move in and help take care of her while her health declined. She would also help take care of Mr. Gilsum, who hadn't so much as made a suitable meal, or washed a load of laundry for himself his entire life. Ben had long feared what would happen to his father if they lost Mrs. Gilsum.

Though he struggled with the idea of Aunt Lilian moving into his room, he saw it as a blessing. The fact that she and Mr. Gilsum fought like cats and dogs for as long as he could remember, a feud that only intensified as the two grew older, didn't bother Ben so much. Especially since he'd moved out of his parents' house. The only concern for Ben now was getting over how creeped out he felt in his new apartment.

"Hello, Dr. Orchard," Ben answered after his ringing cell phone nearly knocked him out of his chair.

"You got my email with the acceptance? That's great. I gave my notice at the plant. I'm all yours in two weeks," Ben continued, after his heartrate decelerated.

"Perfect. You'll assist me for the rest of the fall semester with all of my classes. I'll let you in on all my teaching methods and give you some ideas. Then, if you're up for it, and you better be, you'll teach Early American History during the spring semester. We'll see how you do with that before we load you up the following fall while you complete your master's program," Dr. Orchard announced in an excited voice.

"I'm looking forward to getting started. And I've begun my research on Dr. Joseph Warren. I have some ideas for the journal submission that I'd love to run by you some time."

"Why don't you continue with your research and we'll sit down together to review your notes when you start here in two weeks," Dr. Orchard suggested. "Be careful, Ben. There are hundreds of published articles about Dr. Joseph Warren. You'll need to work hard to stand out, but not in a way that turns off other historians. Don't get wrapped up in fantasy or speculation. If there's no accepted documentation to back up your claims, they didn't happen. So keep those ideas to yourself."

Ben hung up the phone and looked at the pile of books he'd checked out from the library and then the search results on his laptop. *Hundreds? More like thousands.*

The young historian would need to rely on something he believed most of those other writers didn't have. *I'm gonna read all the letters I can find. I already know the history of Dr. Warren. I'm going to get to know the man himself.*

Ben believed he could get a sense of what Dr. Joseph Warren was thinking, even feeling, by reading his letters. And that would give him a perspective that no one had been able to properly document before. *But be careful to avoid fantasy. Back it up with history.*

One interesting fact about Dr. Joseph Warren fascinated Ben above all. Warren had a close relationship with the notorious traitor, General Benedict Arnold. There were close friendships between Warren and John and Abigail Adams, and John's cousin Samuel Adams as well. Dr. Warren once saved John's eldest son, John Quincy Adams' finger from amputation. But the relationship with Benedict Arnold stood out to Ben.

When Dr. Joseph Warren fell at Bunker Hill, he left his four children behind. Their mother had already passed and the children were left in peril when they lost their father. Benedict Arnold donated $500 for their education and wrote to Congress, twice, to secure half of a Major General's pay for the children's care until the youngest reached adulthood…

A noise outside disturbed the history lesson. Ben wanted to stop reading and look around, but it was dark outside, and the small windows in his apartment didn't give him much of a view. *Probably just some animal wandering around…*

"What the hell?" Ben yelled to himself after his thoughts were interrupted by a cellphone ringing outside, followed by someone cursing, maybe falling down, and then footsteps running away.

"Who's out here?" Ben asked after he rushed out of his apartment through the art room, to open the door of the old church.

Ben didn't get an answer. The sound of a car door slamming in the distance down North Main Street startled him. The car drove away quickly, tires squealing, without headlights until it sped out of sight.

Chapter 15

Billy Sullivan flew north on Interstate 49. He had waited until he made his way to the interstate to return the phone call that chased him away from his reconnaissance mission at Ben's apartment. The phone call was as much a surprise to Billy as it was to Ben, not because of the timing, but because it came from someone he'd never expected to hear from again. Still, Billy cursed himself for being so carless. *I'm such a fucking idiot. I can't believe I didn't turn my stupid cell phone off.*

"Well, look who's finally answering one of my calls. And only after leaving nine messages," Billy said, excited to get an answer.

"I'm worried about you, Billy. Your last message freaked me out. Why are you in Kansas City? Why the hell are you stalking Ben Gilsum?" Angelina Rindge asked.

"What do you care what I do? And don't tell me you still have feelings for that little rat. Didn't he drop you like a bad habit? I knew you were hurting, but it's been a while now, Angel. I think it's time to get over it."

"I said I'm worried about *you* Billy, not Ben," Angelina lied.

"Right, Angel. I'm supposed to believe that after you ignored all my phone calls?"

"I'm so sorry to hear about your father. You must be hurting pretty bad. I'm here for you," Angel added, changing the subject.

"Thank you. And don't worry about me. I'll be fine. My father and I did very well in DC before the fucking rat ruined everything. I've got a little business to clean up here in the God-forsaken Bible Belt, and then I'm heading back east. Back to civilization."

"Why don't you come home to Boston now? You and I can get together for coffee or something. You could use a friend, right?" Angelina asked, almost dry heaving at the suggestion.

"You're too good to me, beautiful. But I'm not going home until someone pays for what they did to my father. He died out here in the middle of nowhere. And he died alone. My father was a great man. He didn't deserve a fate like that."

"Billy, don't do anything stupid. Ben had nothing to do with your father's death. You told me in one of your messages he died from pancreatic cancer."

"Who said I was going after Ben? You're not gonna be a rat, too, are you? Are you gonna try and warn your old boyfriend? You do still have feelings for him, don't you?" Billy pressed her impatiently.

"He hasn't spoken to me since I left Washington. He made it pretty clear then he doesn't want anything to do with me. I doubt he'd even answer if I called. Billy, I'm trying to keep *you* out of trouble."

"Well, thank you for your concern, Angel. But like I said, I'll be fine. There's nothing here for me anyway, now that my father's gone. Our contact out here won't work with me without my dad being part of it. He was supposed to set us up again, keep us busy. Since my father got sick he's been ignoring me completely. I've been wasting away in this shithole for way too long. Believe me, I wanna get out of here as soon as possible. I finally got the asshole contact to agree to see me tomorrow, but I don't think much is gonna come from it. Probably just a sweet see ya later. Once that's done, and I take care of a rat problem, I'll come back to Boston. It would be great to see you again."

Angelina didn't answer. A feeling of sadness overwhelmed her as she thought about Ben Gilsum. *He has no idea what's coming his way. I need to do something.*

"Did you mean it when you said you wanted to see me?" Billy asked in a softer, less macho tone.

"Sure, Billy. But only if you keep away from Ben. I don't have any feelings for him, I promise. But if you go after him, I'm afraid I'll never see you again. You'll end up getting locked away out there, in that shithole, as you put it. And if anyone finds out that I knew you were going after him, and I didn't do anything about it, I'd be joining you."

"Oh, I wouldn't worry too much about that. You should see where he's staying. He's literally in the middle of nowhere. A bomb could go off in his lap, and it'd take an hour for anyone to notice."

"Billy, think about what I said before you do anything. I mean it. OK?"

"Well, anyway Angel, thanks for returning my call, finally. I'll see you real soon, beautiful girl. Don't be a stranger," Billy said before hanging up the phone.

Chapter 16

Billy Sullivan drove past GG's Barbacoa Café in Kansas City, Kansas twice before he finally realized he'd arrived at the right place. *You've got to be fucking kidding me.*

The small café had a sign out front made from white-painted plywood and red letters. *Well, that's pretty fucking classy.* He parked in one of only five spots in front of the building, which shared a small potholed parking lot with the neighboring auto mechanic shop. Billy's Mercedes S-Class Sedan, and Doug Tamworth's Lexus LS 500 looked completely out of place. And not just because they both had out-of-state plates.

Billy ran a nervous hand through his slicked back hair, straightened his expensive suit, and went inside where he found Doug sitting at a table, waving him down.

"Boy, you really know how to pick em', Doug. You sure you couldn't have found a more uptown place? Something in Kansas City, *Missouri* maybe?" Billy asked, shaking his head as he sat down across from Doug, who was dressed in jeans with sneakers.

The tall, thin blond man, with gold, round-framed glasses wore a sport coat over a dress shirt with no tie. Doug was fifty-six years old, but looked like a man not a day over forty. He shared his ninety-nine-year-old grandfather's genes, or perhaps his fountain of youth. He tended to squint his eyes when he spoke. The mannerism earned him an insulting nickname from Billy, who often referred to him as the weasel.

"This place has the best Mexican food and barbeque around. Give it a chance. Try the beef barbacoa omelette. It'll change your entire perception of the West," Doug answered.

"The Mid-West is a shithole. And this place is a dump. I think I'll just have a cup of coffee," Billy said to a waitress who appeared almost too stunned and offended to ask Doug what he'd be having.

"Well then. Let's get right down to business. I picked this place because you and I should never be seen together. The fallout of our relationship going public would not only put my legal career in jeopardy, it would crush my grandfather. Those things matter, Billy. More than anything. Which is why I agreed to meet with you. We need to talk about our relationship, and the future."

"This should be a fun conversation," Billy answered, looking around the café with a disgusted expression.

"You know, your father and I met at this place when you two first arrived out here. He liked it. He liked the local flavor of it. Bradford always did appreciate things like that. He was a good man," Doug said in a soft tone.

Billy didn't respond. He just stared into his coffee cup as he stirred in three teaspoons of sugar.

"There are a couple of very important things I need to ask you. Demand of you, actually. First, stop calling me with your cell phone. Your activities in Washington, DC over the past few years may be clear of scrutiny from the feds, thanks to your father, but don't be naïve enough to think no one is paying attention anymore. Second, and this is more for you than me, stay away from Ben Gilsum. And driving out there, to Decatur, with the same cell phone you've been calling me with is reckless. You should know better than that by now. I wouldn't be surprised if you're already under surveillance."

"Those assholes don't care what happens out here. No one is watching me," Billy declared, finally looking into Doug's eyes.

"I can't believe how much you still have to learn. I know your father taught you better. This is not the way we handle our business. Billy, listen to me on this. You have so much more to lose than to gain by going after Ben Gilsum." Doug was losing his patience.

"How about you leave my father out of the rest of this conversation?" Billy requested in a cold, serious tone.

"Very well. Then there's only one thing left to say. Our association ends right here. I can't help you anymore. We need to cut ties completely."

"I already planned on that. I just wanted to let you know I'll be heading back east soon. As soon as I take care of a mutual irritation. You know, the rat? That hick, who now holds the position with the Brothers of Herrad you've been craving your entire life? The current Worshipful Master, Ben Gilsum," Billy declared foolhardily.

"For God's sake, lower your voice. I do want to be Worshipful Master, that's no secret. But I don't want you doing anything stupid. I brought you and your father into the Brothers because I knew how much funding you two could provide and how much influence came with Bradford Sullivan. Your father's influence helped our organization become extremely powerful. I don't regret being involved with Bradford Sullivan in any way. Don't make me start to," Doug warned.

A laugh from Billy was the only response.

"If you do something foolish, everything your father built for you is gone. The agreement to let you two slip away unscathed is over. You lose everything, Billy."

"I've already lost everything. I feel useless out here. I'll never find a job that I'll feel alive doing again. You know, I thought you'd be happy to hear that I was taking care of the rat. I'm doing you a favor," Billy said with a forced smile.

"You're wrong. It's only a matter of time until Ben quits the Brothers. He never wanted to be a leader, of anything. I knew that the day I gave him the book and the ring in Decatur at the request of my grandfather. Wait, Billy. Do me that one favor. Wait for him to quit. In the meantime, you and I need to dissolve our relationship completely. We don't know each other, and we've never met," Doug declared.

"Fine. I don't know you. I never knew you. I'll never contact you again," Billy agreed.

The young man stood up, ready to leave. "I'll give you one month. I spooked the bastard anyway, and lost the element of surprise. In one month, after he's sure everything is safe and cozy in Decatur again, I'm getting my revenge. I don't care about the fallout. You figure that part out. You're the fucking lawyer." Billy stomped out of the café.

Doug Tamworth calmly finished his breakfast, paid the bill, and walked out to his car. The call he made from the stored contacts on his cell before pulling away and heading east, back to Missouri was brief.

"This is Doug Tamworth. You were right. We can't control Billy now that Bradford's gone. The kid's gonna wind up getting arrested and that puts all of us at risk. We need to intervene. We have thirty days. When he falls apart, we need to make certain he's not taken alive."

Chapter 17

It felt unusual, yet comforting, driving to work without his dad sitting next to him. Ben was excited for his first day as an official employee of John Brown University. *I actually thought I'd miss the old man. Breathing heavily. Ignoring me. All the way to work. Good for me, I guess I don't.*

As he often did, to clear his mind while driving to the company in Washington, DC, Ben turned up the radio and sang along, loudly. He could never get away with doing so on the DC Metro, nor in Decatur with his father in the old Chevy pickup.

The ride south, from Decatur to Siloam Springs, Arkansas, on the Arkansas-Oklahoma border, took about twenty minutes. Most of the ride on Arkansas Highway 59 was filled with wide-open green fields. The scenery here looked far less active than the scenery from Mount Vernon, Virginia along the Potomac. But it relaxed the young Assistant Professor and made him feel at home.

Ben found his way to Dr. Orchard's office easily having become familiar with its location as a student years earlier. The shy young man approached the open door slowly, peeking inside. Dr. Orchard was reading a newspaper and drinking coffee. The reading glasses that he called his cheaters were dropped low on his nose to allow him to see clearly while looking down at his paper.

Ben knocked gently on the doorframe to keep from startling the man. "Good morning, Dr. Orchard."

Dr. Orchard looked up and took off his cheaters to toss them on his desk. "Mr. Gilsum. It's terrific to see you."

"It's terrific to be here, Sir."

"That, my dear friend and soon to be colleague, better be the last time you look at me and utter the word 'Sir'. That is unless the Queen of England fulfills my life-long dream and makes me a knight."

Ben laughed a little too much and then answered, "Forgive me, Dr. Orchard. I'm just the new guy. I'll come around."

"You most certainly will. Now, before we do anything, there is someone who insisted on welcoming you the moment you arrived. We need to go and say hello to the president of the university. You remember her, don't you? Dr. Chipman-Young or President Chip as she's affectionately known by our students."

Ben had only met Pamela Chipman-Young one time during his four years at JBU, when she shook his hand at graduation. He remembered Dean Gross telling him with a wink during his job interview that she liked Ben. And he didn't understand why. However, the young interviewee didn't waste time trying to figure it out. He had more important things to be concerned about.

Dr. Chipman-Young stood as Ben and Dr. Orchard entered her office. She had a tiny frame, under five feet tall. She wore her long dark hair up, pulled into a careful bun. She spoke deliberately, in an elegant and captivating tone. She looked like a Halfling when she stood next to Ben and Dr. Orchard who were both over six feet tall. She was a brilliant educator and administrator. Though quiet and humble in appearance, she was fierce when it came to doing what she believed best for her beloved students and university.

"Hello, Benjamin David. It's so nice to see you again," Dr. Chipman-Young said as she shook Ben's hand.

Benjamin David? Oh God, please don't call me…

"I'm sure you don't remember, Mr. Gilsum, but I met you long before you became a student here. When you were very young, no more than five or six. Your Aunt Lillian used to bring you to the First Baptist Church in Decatur where my husband gave sermons on occasion. My oldest daughter volunteered to help in the children's room, where the younger children played during church services."

Ben remembered going to the First Baptist Church a few times with his Aunt Lilian. *I only went for the free donuts.*

"She told me I just had to see this beautiful, shy, young boy named Benjamin David. She also said you only came to church for the free donuts, by the way," Dr. Chipman-Young added with a smile.

Oops. Busted.

"You were reading a book, quietly in a corner, while all the other children ran around like wild animals."

Ben remembered how much he loathed being called Benjamin David, which only happened at the First Baptist Church in the children's room. He hated it only slightly more than being called Benjamin, but it was well worth it for a free donut. He went every Sunday during the summer as a six year old with his aunt, but he didn't remember Dr. Chipman-Young, or her daughter.

"I was an English Literature professor here at the time, and I introduced myself to you. I shook your hand and told you how nice it would be if you continued to read like you were. I said you could eventually become one of my favorite students. Of course, by the time you arrived here, I'd become president of the university. But I knew who you were when you arrived, and it made me smile all the same. I never got a chance to tell you this story while you were a student here. Imagine my delight to welcome you today. Taking the first steps on the path to becoming a professor. Welcome home, Mr. Gilsum, it's a great joy to have you."

Chapter 18

A room that had obviously been a closet with just enough space for a desk and metal, two-drawer file cabinet was the next stop on Ben's first morning at JBU. He felt a wave of schoolboy excitement wash over him when he saw it. *I didn't think I'd actually have an office.*

"A modest beginning, my friend. In due time, I'll remind you of the look I'm seeing on your face right now. You and I will share a good laugh about this humble little office," Dr. Orchard declared with a gentle pat on Ben's back.

"This will do just fine until then," Ben answered before realizing the office didn't come with a computer or phone.

"Your computer is on order, and maintenance will have a phone installed by the end of the week. Don't worry about that. We'll start you out easy. You don't need those things yet," Dr. Orchard added, noticing Ben's somewhat puzzled look.

Ben nodded, but wondered what he'd be doing in his office until his computer arrived. *Should I count the scuff marks on the plain white walls?*

"How about today you spend some time with me in my office? I have a class in two hours. Your class, next semester, Early

American History. You can sit in and watch me work. We'll have lunch and I'll go over the rest of the syllabus with you. You can catch up and begin to participate when you're ready. If I recall correctly, you made some progress on your paper about Dr. Warren? We can discuss that now, while we wait to go to class," Dr. Orchard suggested.

The two made their way back to Dr. Orchard's office and Ben sat down in a chair in front of the professor's desk. It was the same seat he took as a student a couple years earlier while meeting with his professor to discuss his thesis paper on the same subject.

"OK, Mr. Gilsum. Tell me what you have so far. Don't hold anything back. You're not being graded this time. This time it's personal. What can you tell me about Dr. Joseph Warren that a hundred other historians haven't already told me?"

"Well, the first thousand words or so are a summary of facts you've probably heard already."

"No. Don't bore me with that. You can safely assume the people who will read this journal submission already know all of those things as well. Start with the good stuff," Dr. Orchard demanded.

Ben showed a little frustration, shook his head and shuffled around the papers he'd pulled out of his leather messenger bag. *Well, that just cut my article in half.*

"OK, well, most historians probably don't know how close Dr. Warren and Benedict Arnold were. The two were good friends.

I've read several letters between them, and they clearly developed a personal bond with one another. Both were Freemasons and original members of the Sons of Liberty. They were both spectacular personalities."

"That's better, Mr. Gilsum. Start your journal submission with that, please. Sprinkle in a summarized version of the basic history you intended to start with after, and throughout if you must. Explain, in detail, what you mean about spectacular personalities. Add a bunch of stuff about his being a Freemason. People love the mysterious stuff. But don't go beyond the facts. This isn't a novel."

"Well, Dr. Warren was appointed Grand Master of all Scottish Freemasonry in the thirteen colonies. The same group where Paul Revere was Secretary of the Lodge," Ben added.

"Good stuff. Add as much as you can about the known facts surrounding that group, Scottish Freemasonry, who belonged to it and such. Even history going back before the colonies would be useful. It's interesting."

"I intend to. And perhaps some discussion of how the Freemasons influenced the founding of our country. I'd like to use that information to further discuss how many of the more powerful forefathers were also Freemasons and how well-respected Dr. Warren was among them. There are quotes from some extremely influential people of the day who believed Dr. Warren would have been the first president of the United States if he'd survived the Revolutionary War. Though I'd not be the first person to make that point," Ben admitted.

"That's speculation. It may be OK, it's interesting, but only if you back it up with facts. I'm not sure about it, though, I'll have to think about it some more. You need all of those quotes to be included and verified by more than one source."

"Dr. Warren had relationships with British sympathizers, too, but that wasn't uncommon among the founding fathers. They maintained business and social relationships with very powerful people, on both sides of the conflict. I could tie that into some of the Benedict Arnold stuff, but I'm not suggesting anything dark about Dr. Joseph Warren."

"Good. Don't. Be very careful about venturing into fantasy land. If you take a wild or unpopular stand on this subject, you could ruin your reputation before it has a chance to blossom."

"I considered *some* speculation about the direction Warren may have taken the country if he were elected to be the first president. Perhaps a change from some of the precedents that were set by Washington," Ben said.

"I don't like speculation. It's unwise to presume you know what direction Dr. Warren may have taken the new country in. I'd avoid that speculation entirely."

"In regard to speculation, I have to insist you allow me just a small amount of latitude on the topic of Benedict Arnold. It's kind of an important part of my submission. It has a lot to do with how Dr. Warren influenced those around him. How he may have been the missing, positive influence Benedict Arnold needed," Ben declared.

I read the letters. I got a strong sense of what the man was thinking. A sense of what he was made of. Of course no one will understand how, but I did. I need to make them believe me somehow. I'll figure that part out as I go. I hope.

"I'm listening. Proceed with caution, Mr. Gilsum."

"Well, I'm not about to suggest Dr. Warren could have been a traitor. Not even close. Please don't get me wrong. My theory, if you will, is that if Warren survived the Battle of Bunker Hill and acquired the combat experience he desired, it's possible, based on documented accounts of how the men who fought by his side instinctively followed him without knowing his rank, he may have been able to influence Arnold to remain loyal to the colonials. I understand this is speculation, but it's speculation based on some fact and recorded history. It also portrays Dr. Warren in a positive manner."

"I may be able to allow that much speculation, but something tells me you want to take it a bit further. What else have you got in mind?"

"Both men, according to letters and accounts from people who knew them, were true patriots. Both honorable. Though there were some complaints about Arnold from his peers. Corruption charges that were ultimately dismissed," Ben admitted.

Dr. Orchard tilted his head to one side and nodded with a grin.

Ben continued, "The war was long and difficult, on everyone. There are accounts mentioning doubt and despair from some of the most notable founding fathers. And the Americans didn't exactly crush the British per many historical records. They merely survived them long enough to win some key battles near the end of the war. They out willed them."

"Nothing that justifies or excuses betrayal then?" Dr. Orchard asked.

The young assistant professor ignored the question and continued, "It's widely accepted that Arnold turned traitor because he felt frustrated about his lack of recognition for being a prominent member of the Sons of Liberty. He'd been passed for promotion. He had enormous debts to pay. He was injured and could hardly walk, rendering him less useful in the mind of the colonial leaders. Or his wife was a loyalist. There's a list of reasons and Benedict Arnold never had a perfect reputation away from the battlefield. I think it's at least possible Arnold turned traitor because he couldn't stand the reality of a prolonged war. I believe he'd lost his will to fight."

That's the impression I get from reading his letters anyway. I just can't explain how or why I have that impression.

"You're treading on dangerous ground. Still, I'm at least intrigued by your theory. Please remind me again how this bit about Benedict Arnold has anything to do with Dr. Joseph Warren."

"Like I said before, a close friendship with someone with as much resolve and honor as Warren could have been enough to inspire Benedict Arnold to stay the course," Ben added with a smile, hoping his new mentor would agree.

"If you can write this in a way that uses documented fact to back up your conclusions, and admit it's only speculation, not being presented as a suggestion of fact, I might offer my blessing. I need to see how you present your theory first. Right now I'm not sure if I'm impressed by your insight, or disappointed by your drift into fantasy land. Your rough draft will help me make that determination."

Ben responded with a look of disgruntlement. *He wants new ideas, but zero speculation. He wants to be inspired, but without original thought. This is hopeless.*

Dr. Orchard picked up on Ben's distress. "Don't get frustrated, my friend. People like you and I have to avoid emotional reactions, or wild theories that can't be proven easily. I'm protecting you from the wolves that will read your journal submission, and do their best to declare you a fool to the entire academic community. I'd proceed with caution about taking a sympathetic stand toward one of the most hated figures in American History. A notorious traitor."

Ben sat there speechless, unable to explain why he believed in his theory. *George Washington trusted the man implicitly. A lot of others did, too. He was a hero before he turned, and he wasn't alone in considering it.*

Dr. Orchard continued, "I already know you're more gifted than most of the country's respected historians. If you'll take my advice, if you do this right, they'll all know it, too."

Chapter 19

A frustrated but determined Ben Gilsum gathered all the notes for his article and put them with all the other papers and documents back into his leather messenger bag. He took a short walk to his new office and dropped the bag on his empty desk. It was time to sit in on Dr. Orchard's lecture for the Early American History class. The conversation about his paper was running endlessly through his mind. *I'm going to write this paper my way, with my ideas and my theories. And I'll do it in a way that wins Dr. Orchard's blessing, of course…*

Dr. Orchard told his new hire not to take any notes during the lecture. He didn't want Ben to look like a new student. "I'll introduce you to the class, and then you can observe. Pay close attention. Get some ideas, perhaps," the professor instructed.

Ben sat quietly during the lecture, looking down at the syllabus Dr. Orchard provided. A few of the students were staring at him, wondering how someone barely older than them could have been hired to teach at JBU. *HST 2113 United States History to 1865. My favorite period of American history.*

Ben sat there, daydreaming. Barely paying attention as Dr. Orchard discussed the early days of the Civil War.

The Assistant Professor's mind wandered away from the lecture, which he already knew he could easily give himself. His thoughts drifted to the Brothers of Herrad. Though he had dedicated space in the old church for the new lodge, Ben was feeling guilty for doing little else for the organization he'd agreed to lead.

I don't have any ideas about recruiting members, or projects to help the community, or anything else. I wonder if I should ask some of the professors here if they want to consider membership. I know some of Dad's friends at the plant would be interested. Dr. Orchard maybe? I bet he'd get a kick out of the group.

Ben quickly gathered himself as the lecture came to an end and made sure his boss knew he was paying attention, offering an occasional nod and grin. As the students were dismissed, Dr. Orchard offered to buy lunch at Ziggywurst, a German inspired restaurant that had opened just two years earlier about a mile from campus in Siloam Springs.

Ziggywhat?

Sitting across from each other at Ziggywurst Ben looked over the unfamiliar menu. *What's the difference between a wurst and a schnitzel?*

He decided to take a leap of faith and ordered a jalapeno chicken wurst with sauerkraut, chips, and a pickle. "Hold the onions please."

"So, Ben, what are you doing with your free time over in Decatur?" Dr. Orchard asked, to start conversation.

"You may recall I talked a little about it in my interview with you and Dr. Gross. I'm a month or so away from opening a boys and girls club in town. It's a place for kids to come and hang out, play games, participate in reading and art projects. Stay out of trouble mostly and build some friendships and confidence. All for no cost," Ben answered, proudly.

"I remember. That sounds terrific, Ben. Very impressive. How do you get funding for a project like that? Is it church affiliated? You know a Christian University like JBU could be a possible sponsor. We love getting involved in things like that," Dr. Orchard offered.

"Actually, I've been working with various businesses around town. The response has been great. But most of my funding comes from my association with a fraternal organization."

"You mean like a social club. An Elks Lodge or some veteran's group? You're not a veteran," the professor added.

"More like a private society. Similar to the Freemasons. We're called the Brothers of Herrad. I'll bet you've never heard of us."

"I've heard plenty about the Freemasons, but I'm afraid I know nothing about the Brothers of Herrad. What's that all about?"

"We dedicate our lives to helping others. We raise money for local community needs. We volunteer time for the service of children or people who could use a little help. I like to think of us as an adult Boy Scout troop."

"Sounds interesting," Dr. Orchard replied, but Ben sensed the professor was losing interest.

"It's funny that we're talking about this," Ben said. "I've been thinking about trying to recruit you as a member."

Dr. Orchard paused and thought about what Ben said before answering. "A couple years ago someone approached me about joining the Freemasons. I declined. I used the excuse that I worked for a Christian University and my superiors would frown on my being involved with a secret society. Of course, though some of them may disagree, the university doesn't require students or teachers to belong to any specific religion. As you know, we attend services and agree to live our lives in accordance with the Christian faith, but that's the only requirement. It was an easy way for me to say no politely."

"So are you still not interested in joining a group like ours?" Ben persisted.

"Well, Ben, I do admire you and your organization for your service to the community. But for me, it's a pass. I'll continue to volunteer with my church, and donate money through them. I worry that secret societies…"

"Private societies," Ben interrupted.

Dr. Orchard humored his young friend. "Right, private societies. These private societies, though well intentioned, tend to cause members to over aggrandize their position in the community. Maybe even cause them to believe they've become somehow better than others. I think they tend to believe we're all here to serve some greater purpose in life. Greater even than just being a good and faithful individual. For me, Mr. Gilsum, being a good person, a faithful husband, father and grandfather, a good Christian, and of course a good teacher, helping young minds to appreciate the value of history, is all I need in this life. Those things have always been more than enough for me. That's my purpose, and that's what makes me feel accomplished."

The professor's answer had made the young man stop and think about his own experiences and his own reluctance to continue being a member of the Brothers. *Is it enough to be a good person? A good teacher? I'll be starting a boys and girls club, too. We can do volunteer work around town with the kids. Do I really even want to run a Brothers of Herrad lodge?*

Chapter 20

Ben settled in quickly at John Brown University and he was anxious to begin teaching his own classes. Dr. Orchard insisted on a pace that felt too slow and Ben was left with more free time at work than he knew what to do with.

In his spare time, the reluctant Worshipful Master, and only member of the Decatur, Arkansas lodge of the Brothers of Herrad came up with an idea to spark interest in the organization around town. Ben needed to do something that would make an impression so he could finally begin to recruit new members. *I've been putting this off long enough. Time to make good on my promise to Mr. James. If I pull this off, people are gonna want to be a part of the Brothers for sure.*

During his dealings with City Hall to get the Decatur Club for Boys and Girls started, a clerk showed Ben the Community Room. The room was available for rent to citizens of Decatur, at low rates, for functions and meetings. The town made good use of the space, like hosting the Annual Decatur Barbeque.

Ben noticed the room, a basketball court covered with tables and chairs, needed some type of decoration or color. The very tall walls around the Community Room were covered with wood paneling on the bottom that rose about three feet up from the floor. The rest of the walls stretched to the high ceiling, covered with nothing but white paint. *This room could use some color. Maybe something with a little local flavor.*

A brainstorming session with his mother produced a fundraising idea. Mrs. Gilsum, the former, favorite elementary school teacher and active PTA member, reminded her son of a beloved tradition in Decatur that had ended years ago.

"Oh, we used to have town dances when I was a young girl. We'd sell baked goods all day, and play games with the children. Then in the evening we'd have music and dancing. We did this anytime the town needed to raise money for anything," Mrs. Gilsum recalled.

At first Ben scoffed at the suggestion. *A bake sale? I'm going to raise money for the town with a bake sale?*

But then he had a thought. "What if we held the bake sale at the club? The fields are ready. Kids and parents could play games outside. We could set up the art room to sell baked goods. We could easily set up a dance on the basketball court. What do you think, Mom? Just like old times?"

"Oh, my goodness baby, that's a wonderful idea. The town is going to love you for this. I can make my peach cobbler, and I'll spread the word to all the folks around town. I'm not the only person in Decatur who has a famous baked recipe. Wait until I tell the ladies at the PTA. This will be lovely."

"We can promote the Brothers of Herrad as the sponsor of the event, and also give everyone a peek at the Decatur Club for Boys and Girls. I know people are curious about the place. This will make them feel right at home," Ben added with enthusiasm.

"What do you plan on doing with the money you raise, exactly? Are you just painting the Community Room? It won't take much to accomplish that."

"Oh, no, Mom. Better than just a paint job. Bigger. You know the train parked off the tracks, over by the depot museum on South Main?"

"Of course I do. That's a treasured landmark here in Decatur. The Kansas City Southern."

"Right. Well how would you like to see that beautiful red, black, and yellow train painted over the bare white walls of the Community Room? I know an artist from John Brown. She's a teacher and we've become friends. She's already offered to volunteer, and work with kids at the club when it opens. She has a great heart. She'll do the work for the cost of paint, and I've offered to pay her a small fee. We'll need to sell a fair amount of cakes and cookies, though. Do you think we can do it?"

"That would be perfect. And I know we can do it. Baby, if you can make both of these things happen the town would be forever grateful. I'm gonna cry just thinking about it. Simply wonderful."

The Kansas City Southern locomotive and caboose was now retired and parked next to a train station that was transformed into a museum. The prominent locomotive was painted yellow on the roof and around the windows, with a thick red stripe through the middle, and painted black along the bottom, outlined in yellow with the words "Kansas City Southern." The image of the beloved landmark and picturesque station were exactly what the Community Room walls needed.

For the first time since accepting the ring of the Worshipful Master, Ben felt confident about his new role with the Brothers. *This is going to be the perfect welcoming party for both the club and the Brothers of Herrad. Now I just have to hope Mom and her friends from the PTA can deliver the baked goods.*

Chapter 21

Angelina Rindge relaxed in the sun room, watching The View, on the Friday before Thanksgiving, taking a much needed break from law school to spend some time with her family for the week. Marta invited her to go shopping with her in preparation for the upcoming feast, but Angelina declined. She just wanted to veg out and do nothing for a few hours.

"Veg out? What the heck is that? You can veg out with me. I'll be buying plenty of vegetables for you to veg out on," Marta replied.

"No, thank you, Marta. I just wanna *relax.* I should be reading law books, but I'll do that some other time. Maybe we can go out for a drink later? I'll whine to you about how hard my finals are gonna be."

"That sounds horrible. I'm in. See you later, procrastinator," Marta announced and left Angelina alone to relax.

Soon after Marta left, the doorbell rang. Angelina ignored it, but a few moments later it rang again. *So much for vegging out.*

"Angelina Rindge? I'm FBI Special Agent Reina Dario," a square-jawed woman announced, showing her badge for Angelina to see.

Angelina hoped someone would be coming to speak with her, but she was surprised it happened so quickly. She'd called the Decatur Police Department immediately after her phone conversation with Billy Sullivan regarding the threatening messages he left about Ben. Decatur Police called her back, after speaking with her, and informed her there was an FBI investigation in progress. They said she should expect an agent to contact her soon.

Special Agent Reina Dario looked like a superhero to Angelina. She appeared strong, physically fit, probably in her late twenties. She stood as tall as Angelina, with perfect posture. She wore her short, brown hair cropped, military-style and spoke in short, direct sentences, never straying off topic. No small talk. Angelina admired her immediately. *She's a badass.*

"Do you have some time to talk with me about a mutual friend? Ben Gilsum?" Agent Dario asked.

Angelina invited the special agent into her parents' home. "You know Ben?"

"I do. We worked together in Washington, DC, for a short time before he left. Ben is a good person. I liked him very much. I'm here to talk with you about your phone call to the Decatur Police Department. Our friend may be in trouble."

Angelina wanted to know more about Agent Dario's relationship with Ben, "So did you guys work in the same office together? I don't really know how Ben's job worked. He never gave any details. Come to think of it, that's kinda his style, right? No details, about anything. Unless of course it's some historical monument or statue," Angelina added with a laugh that quickly felt a little uncomfortable due to Agent Dario's dry expression.

"I worked directly for the Federal Government. Ben's former company is a private contractor. Ben reported to me, only as required, about specific communications he was tasked to analyze. I'm a field agent now, so we wouldn't have any contact if Ben stayed with the company. During his tenure there, Ben knew me as Ms. Green."

"So, you were Ben's boss?" Angelina persisted.

"No," Special Agent Dario answered, quickly changing the subject and getting to business. "If you don't mind, I'd like to ask you some questions about your connection with William Sullivan."

"Billy, yeah. Well, he and I were friends from high school and college. We didn't go to the same schools, I lived out here and he lived in South Boston, but we hung around the same places in the city. We even dated for a short time, but that ended badly. I worked in Washington around the same time as he and Ben did. We had a falling out in DC and I stopped talking to him. Then he started calling me a few weeks ago and leaving me messages. I never answered or returned any of his calls. The messages started to get dark and threatening toward Ben. That's when I called the police."

"You did call William before calling the police."

"Right. I did. I tried to talk some sense into him. I even offered to see him. To try and get him away from Ben. Ben and I dated in Washington. I care a lot about him."

"I'm aware of your relationship with Ben. I'm more curious about your current relationship with William."

"Honestly, there is no current relationship with Billy. I would never have even called him if he wasn't threatening Ben. I swear," Angelina declared.

"I believe that, Ms. Rindge. But do you believe William, Billy, still trusts you? Would he continue to talk with you about what he's doing down in Kansas City and Decatur?"

"Yeah, I think he would. I mean he already told me he was going after Ben. I never told him I was gonna call the cops."

"Would you be willing to work with the FBI to gather more information about Billy's plans?"

"I would do anything to protect Ben. Whatever you need me to do, I'm there. Shouldn't you go to Ben now? Is someone there to protect him?"

"I'm flying to Kansas City this evening and assembling a team immediately. We received a tip that Ben would be safe for at least a month. We plan to be there well before then," Agent Dario answered.

"What do you want me to do?" Angelina asked eagerly.

"For now, nothing. I'll leave you my contact information. If Billy reaches out to you again, answer the call. Get him to talk about Ben. Write down everything he says and call me immediately after, no matter what time it is. I'll pick up. If we decide to bring you in, to help us, I'll give you clear instruction."

"I can do that," Angelina agreed. *Write it down? I'm sure they're listening to Billy's calls. She knew I called him. Heck they're probably listening to mine as well by now. She probably already knows everything I just told her. She probably knows what happened between me and Ben, too.*

"One more thing, Ms. Rindge. Don't attempt to contact Ben Gilsum about any of this. We have him protected. I want him to remain calm and proceed as normal. We don't want to risk making Billy suspicious," Agent Dario requested.

Angelina answered softly, with pain in her tone, "Ben hasn't spoken to me since I left Washington. I'm sure he wouldn't answer even if I did call him."

Chapter 22

Mr. Gilsum held the stepladder steady as Ben gently stapled the electrical cord of a string of white Christmas lights around the basketball court at the Decatur Club for Boys and Girls. The lights created a nice atmosphere for the town dance, which would take place immediately following children's games and bake sale, to raise funds to paint the Community Room. Round tables and chairs surrounded the dancefloor, where guests could eat and relax.

Ben put a small square table next to the dancefloor, complete with two large donation jars, and intended to sit there to perform DJ duties. Labels on both jars read, "Decatur Dance Under the Stars. An Introduction to the Decatur Club for Boys and Girls. Sponsored by the Decatur chapter of the Brothers of Herrad. All bake sale proceeds and donations to be used to paint the walls of the Community Room."

Mrs. Gilsum, her friends from the PTA, and Aunt Lilian were busy arranging tables of baked goods, snacks, and drinks in the art room. The men exchanged smiles and a laugh each time they overheard Mrs. Gilsum say, "Oh, my goodness, that's just lovely."

Mr. Gilsum agreed to run the grill, cooking hot dogs, hamburgers, and barbequed chicken for all who came hungry. Many who brought baked goods also provided side dishes. Mr. Gilsum positioned the grill as far away from the bake sale as he possibly could, but Ben asked him to move it a little closer before he started it up.

"Son, this grill is my safe zone," Mr. Gilsum declared.

"Safe zone? What the heck are you talking about Dad?"

"I'm gonna spend as much time cookin' over here as I can. The smoke bothers your Aunt Lilian. Probably 'cause she's a witch, and she's afraid of fire. She'll stay away from it, and by the grace of God, she'll stay away from me. So, if you see me pourin' a little water over the coals on occasion, to get more smoke goin', do me a favor, Son, and don't ask why. You don't know what kinda hell I'm livin' in over at the house. I got two of 'em now, houndin' after me every day. And one of 'em, I swear to you, boy, is a she-devil."

Ben tried not to laugh loud enough for his aunt and mother to hear him, and helped his father move the grill to a more strategic location to the party.

"You keep that devil talk on the down low, Dad, or she's gonna drag your sorry butt into church on Sunday. Believe me. I've been there," Ben warned with a wry smile.

"Like hell she is. If she dragged my sorry butt in there, they'd kick my sorry butt out fast as lightnin'."

More laughter as father and son found the perfect spot for Mr. Gilsum's safe zone. "That should do it, Dad. I think we're actually gonna pull this thing off tonight. I've posted signs all over town, talked to business owners, and spread the word. Everyone seems pretty excited about it."

"And judging by the gaggle of gigglin' ladies carryin' on over yonder, betcha they all intend to drag their poor husbands out onto this here dancefloor. All of 'em, not includin' the she-devil. Ain't nobody in Benton County dumb enough to marry her."

"Don't worry, Dad. Mom knows neither of us likes to dance. I've promised her one slow dance. You better be ready to offer the same, old man."

"Mmm-Hmm. I reckon I better."

The first of many families, with young children, arrived in the early afternoon. The weather cooperated perfectly, offering a beautiful and cloudless seventy-two degree day with a low of sixty-eight expected for the early evening. A warm night in Decatur for November.

Ben showed the families around the art room and offered a tour of the rest of the building. Once enough kids arrived and everyone had a chance to shop the bake sale, the excited club owner announced a game of kickball would be taking place on one of the fields in ten minutes. Mrs. Gilsum took on duties as tour guide after Ben ran off with an enthusiastic group of children.

The sound of Mrs. Gilsum's "Oh, my goodness, that's just lovely," could be heard many times over the course of the afternoon.

As the sun set and the fields became too dark for games, Ben turned on the *stars* over the dancefloor and began to play music. The sound system consisted of nothing more than Ben's laptop playing an iTunes playlist he and his mother had created over a set of speakers he purchased from Best Buy. *It actually sounds better than I expected.*

Mrs. Gilsum was the first person on the dancefloor, waving her arms to her friends and neighbors to join her, which they did.

Ben felt a sense of adoration as he watched his mother pulling old couples out of their seats and laughing with them as they made their way out onto the floor. *How could I have ever pulled this off without her? She's amazing.*

Mrs. Gilsum waited until near the end of the evening to approach her son and collect on the dance he promised her. Her face was beaming with pride for what he had accomplished.

"Play the song, Baby. Come on now and make your mother the happiest woman here."

Ben selected the song Mrs. Gilsum requested specifically for their dance and escorted his mother out to the floor. Friends and neighbors made room for the host of the festivities, and his beloved dance partner.

I Hope You Dance, by Lee Ann Womack played as mother and son took their place in the middle of the dancefloor. Several of the ladies from the PTA wiped away tears while Ben danced with his mother.

"Have I ever told you how proud I am of you, baby?"

"Yes, about a million times, Mom. Although you never had to. I've always known it," Ben answered with a smile.

"Make this a million and one. Look around, baby. Look what you did for this town. Look at them smiling and laughing. They'll never forget this."

"I see a few women crying actually."

"Happy tears, baby. All happy tears," Mrs. Gilsum added as she lost her footing and nearly tripped.

"Mom, are you OK?"

"Oh, I'm perfect, baby. This is perfect. You're perfect," Mrs. Gilsum said, finishing up the dance with her son in silence and then taking a seat next to her husband to rest.

Ben sat at the table with his parents to check on his mother and to discuss the results of the bake sale.

"Mom are you going to be all right?"

"Yes, I'm fine. I'll get a good rest tonight and be all better in the morning, baby."

"Well, guys, I gathered up all the money we raised tonight. I'm afraid we barely made enough to cover paint and supplies. I don't mind calling the food and decorations here a donation from the club, but I'm going to have to pay the artist fee out of my own pocket." Ben hoped he was hiding his sense of failure. "And, I don't think I'm cut out to run a Brothers of Herrad lodge. Not one person asked me about the Brothers. Everyone I ask politely tells me no thanks. I don't think anyone here has any interest in being a member."

"Don't be so hard on yourself, baby. What you did here was pure magic. Who cares about the Brothers of Herrad? You've given a beautiful gift to this community. It came from your heart. And I'm not sure your heart is with the Brothers of Herrad anyway. You don't need to lead some *private society* to be a good man. You should be more concerned about this club, these children, and your teaching career. Maybe even going after your Angel again and showing her what a wonderful man you are," Mrs. Gilsum added, unable to stop herself.

Ben didn't say a word. He leaned back in his chair, until its front two legs lifted slightly off the ground, put both hands behind his head and let out a long sigh. *If it weren't for the Brothers of Herrad, there would be no club. And no Angel, most likely. But would that be a loss or a blessing?*

"Isn't that the artist right there? She's coming this way," Mr. Gilsum announced.

Miranda Swanzey and Ben had quickly become good friends at John Brown after Ben accepted the Assistant Professor of History position. The twenty-six-year-old Assistant Professor of Visual Arts sought him out after learning someone close to her own age would finally be working at the university.

Even though the two were an odd pairing, they enjoyed each other's company and spent much of their lunch hours trading stories about their experiences. Ben, the math and science whiz who dressed in slim-fit suits and expensive shoes, could spend an hour describing the significance of a historical monument no one knew existed. And Miranda, in much more casual and comfortable attire, typically a button-down sweater and long skirt with sandals, didn't care much for material things. She wore her long, brown hair in a loose ponytail. She preferred hiking or rock climbing over visiting landmarks when she wasn't painting something incredibly beautiful.

When Miranda learned about the Decatur Club for Boys and Girls she insisted Ben allow her to volunteer to teach art to the children. Ben excitedly agreed, renaming the reading room the art room.

Ben didn't think she was still at the dance. He'd invited her and she showed up alone just after the dancing started. He introduced her to his parents and a few other neighbors then lost track of her. She had planned to check out the club and see how things were going. She explained to everyone how excited she was to do something nice for the town, even though she lived in Siloam Springs.

Ben put all four legs of his chair back on the ground and stood. "Miranda, thanks again for coming. I'm afraid we didn't raise enough money to cover your fee. I'll figure something out…"

Miranda interrupted, "Are you kidding, Ben?"

Ben didn't understand the question. He was too confused to respond, so he just smiled and shrugged at his friend, hoping she would explain.

"This event was awesome. It was like a scene from a movie on the Hallmark Channel. Mrs. Gilsum, you're so beautiful. I cried when you two were dancing. I'm heading home y'all, but listen. I'll paint the Community Room for free, with pleasure. I wasn't planning on accepting the fee you offered anyhow, Ben. I'd really like to be part of this. All I ask is that you let me keep the leftover paint and supplies for my students to use in class. Some of them wanna come along and help me paint. It would be our honor to do something beautiful for Decatur. Sound like a deal?"

"Oh, my goodness, that's just lovely." Mrs. Gilsum declared.

Chapter 23

Everyone left the dance and Ben worked alone, picking up around the old church building. His parents were supposed to help, but Mrs. Gilsum wasn't feeling well, so Mr. Gilsum and Aunt Lilian wanted to get her home to rest. *That might just be the first time I've ever seen those two agree on anything.*

The cleanup didn't appear too difficult, but Ben took his time, losing himself in thought. He couldn't decide if the day should be counted as a success or failure. *It seemed like half the town showed up. That's more than I could have ever hoped for. The response to the club was positively perfect. Plenty of kids and their parents loved it. I'm sure they'll be back when we open. I think I got asked about ninety-seven times when that's gonna be.*

But we only raised a few hundred dollars. Barely enough to buy the materials necessary to paint the Community Room. Thank goodness for Miranda's kind gesture to volunteer her services. And even better, her students want to pitch in.

The list of positive results from the day should have made Ben happy. Still, not one person showed any interest in the Brothers of Herrad, which was Ben's original motivation for putting on the event in the first place.

Is it me? Can they sense my lack of enthusiasm for the Brothers? Should I walk away from the Brothers before I make a fool of myself? Bradford Sullivan brought in millions of dollars as Worshipful Master and I bring in a few hundred bucks with a bake sale. A bake sale. Bradford acted illegally, of course, but still. There's no way I'll ever come close…

The ringing of his cellphone interrupted his thoughts as he put the finishing touches on picking up around the old church. The display showed a local number, but not one on Ben's contact list. *Who the heck would be calling now?*

"Ben, honey. It's Aunt Lilian. I borrowed someone's cellphone. You need to get to Siloam Springs Regional Hospital, right away. It's your mother. She's not doing well."

Ben ran into his apartment, grabbed his keys and left without locking the door.

The hospital lobby was empty except for an elderly woman who yelled after Ben to slow down. As he struggled to catch his breath to ask for information about his mother, Aunt Lilian appeared. She'd been waiting for him to take him to the private waiting room to be with his father.

"Dad what's happening? Where is she? Can we see her?"

Mr. Gilsum looked up at him with tears streaming from his eyes. Ben froze, unable to remember the last time he saw his father cry. Mr. Gilsum didn't say a word. He didn't have to. Ben knew things were bad.

"Your momma was only complaining about feeling tired. We didn't know how bad it was, Ben. She didn't tell us about chest pains, or shortness of breath. She just wanted to lay down," Aunt Lilian explained through her tears.

Ben took a chair across from his father cradling, his forehead in his hands, with his watering eyes dropping tears down his cheeks. *This isn't as bad as they think. She's fine. The doctor's gonna come out here any minute and tell us she's resting. And doing fine.*

Two and a half hours later, just after 1:00 AM, a doctor walked into the waiting room, accompanied by a nurse with tears in her eyes.

"Mr. Gilsum?" The doctor asked.

Ben and his father looked up. The doctor walked over and stood between them.

"I'm sorry, gentlemen. She fought as hard as she could, but her body was weakened due to muscular dystrophy. She had a cardiac arrhythmia, an irregular heartbeat, brought on by her condition, and it worsened over time, eventually leading to heart failure. You mentioned she never complained about chest pains or shortness of breath?" The doctor asked, but no one answered.

The doctor continued, "It's amazing to all of us how hard she must have fought to appear strong. I can only imagine how much difficulty she endured. I'm guessing she wasn't the type of person to complain about much?"

Again no one answered the doctor's question.

Aunt Lilian sobbed loudly.

Mr. Gilsum leaned forward in his chair and buried his face in both of his palms. Ben could only stare in disbelief as his father's shoulders fell under the unimaginable weight of his grief.

"She was obviously an incredibly strong and brave person. I'm so sorry, there wasn't anything more we could have done."

Chapter 24

The morning greeted Ben with a horrible headache, stiff neck, and the sound of Aunt Lilian beating eggs in a bowl in the kitchen. He was forced to sleep on the couch in the living room, because his aunt had moved into his bedroom. He slept terribly, with his head rested on one arm of the couch, while his feet hung nearly a foot over the other. The accommodations weren't ideal, but Ben refused to leave his father alone. *What the hell is she doing in there? Why is she up so early?*

"Well, good morning, sweetie. I made some fresh coffee and there'll be scrambled eggs and toast shortly," Aunt Lilian announced.

"I'd love some coffee, but I'm not hungry. Dad can have my eggs when he wakes up. In an hour. If he'll even want to eat anything."

"You boys are gonna have to eat something. Both of you," Aunt Lilian insisted.

What is wrong with this crazy lady? You can shove those eggs up your ass. Leave me the hell alone.

"That's fine, Aunt Lilian. Thank you. I'll wait for Dad to wake up. If you don't mind, I'll eat with him."

Once Mr. Gilsum came in the three sat together for breakfast in silence. In typical Gilsum fashion, neither of the men spoke about what happened or shared how they were feeling. Aunt Lilian started to cry, but quickly composed herself and wiped her tears away. She knew she'd get little comforting from the Gilsum men. No one spoke until breakfast was finished. Ben helped his aunt pick up and took care of the dishes himself, kissing his aunt on the cheek and thanking her for making breakfast. He felt a little guilty for being bothered earlier by the kind gesture she showed.

Aunt Lilian broke the silence after her nephew came back to the kitchen table. "I plan to stay here with your father. I'll help take care of things around here, now that your momma's gone. I've got nowhere else to go anyhow."

Ben tried to make eye contact with his father, to get an idea of what he thought, but Mr. Gilsum just stared at the coffee cup in front of him. *It's probably for the best. He doesn't even know how to write a check to pay a bill. It's either Aunt Lilian or me. I'm sure Mom would prefer she stick around.*

"Boys, I know this is hard, but we need to discuss arrangements. Funeral and services," Aunt Lilian clarified.

"I'll take care of all of that," Ben declared.

Mr. Gilsum finally broke his silence. "Your mother wants to be laid to rest at Hillcrest Cemetery. The services will be at Epting Funeral Home. Right near the cemetery."

Ben looked at his father, confused. *That tiny place in Gravette? We can do better than that.*

"Son, I can see you don't understand. And you wanna lay your mother to rest someplace upscale and fancy. Maybe in Bentonville or Siloam Springs. But your mother and I spoke on this a short time ago. It's good country in Gravette, and your mother feels comfortable there. It's only a couple miles up the road, and she knew the owner over at Epting. It's what she wants. This is not up for discussion."

"If that's what Mom wants, then that's what she'll get. I'll take care of everything. I want to get her a nice headstone, too. Is there anything either of you want engraved on it?" Ben asked, his voice starting to shake.

"Ben, that's wonderful. Your mother would want it to be simple. How about 'Loving wife, mother, and sister?' I think that says it all," Aunt Lilian suggested.

"Son, you know full well she'd think you're bein' foolish, wastin' all that money on some fancy rock to be put over a grave. But I think that'd be real nice. Real nice, Ben," Mr. Gilsum added.

Chapter 25

Epting Funeral Home, in Gravette, was about seven miles north of Decatur, Arkansas. The roof and most of the exterior walls were covered with aluminum-corrugated siding. Some of the siding still had a light-blue coat of paint while much of it had faded completely in the powerful Arkansas sunshine. The entrance to the building had a tan-brick exterior. Like many buildings in the area, Epting Funeral Home was modest in appearance. And like most owners of surviving businesses in the area, the owner of Epting Funeral Home was local, well-known, and respected by the community.

Mrs. Gilsum's services and calling hours took place in a room barely large enough to fit her casket and twenty-four chairs. There were twelve chairs on each side with a narrow aisle between them, from the doorway to the casket. Ben expected the room to be more than adequate. The only family in attendance were Ben, Mr. Gilsum, and Aunt Lilian. Ben's grandparents had all died before he reached kindergarten. His father was an only child, and Mrs. Gilsum had one sister, Aunt Lilian, who lost her husband before the couple had any children. The Gilsum family had lost touch with any extended relatives many years earlier.

Neither Ben nor his father had any idea how many people were going to come and pay their respects. The line of mourners filled the center aisle in the small room all the way to the front door of the modest building, and continued nearly four hundred feet, to Charlotte Street. The owner of the funeral home loved Mrs. Gilsum too, and allowed extra time for everyone to pay their respects.

Ben shook hands with friends and many unfamiliar faces as they made their way through the room. With tears in his eyes, he offered a barely audible "Thanks for coming," as they passed, hardly making eye contact. Then, a familiar voice caused him to look up in surprise.

"Ben, my son, I'm so sorry for your loss," Mr. James said as he shook his young friend's hand.

Ben had successfully held back tears for most of the day, until the moment he looked up and saw his mentor, for the first time since leaving Washington, DC. The emotion overwhelmed him, and he wrapped his ninety-nine-year-old friend in a hug that nearly knocked him down.

Mr. James looked the same as he did back in Virginia. He even wore the same outfit Ben always remembered seeing him in—wool trousers, dress shirt under a sweater, and sneakers. This time he wore a sport coat. He still smiled, almost constantly, and still shuffled his feet, hardly lifting his sneakers off the ground when he walked.

"I didn't know if I'd ever see you again. There's so much I need to say to you. To thank you for everything. You've given me so much. I don't know where to start," Ben stammered.

"You don't have to thank me for anything. Especially not today. You've given more to me than I could ever return. I don't want to take too much time here. There's probably a hundred and fifty people in line behind me. I'll come and visit with you in a few days, when it's more appropriate to talk," Mr. James promised.

"I look forward to seeing you soon. Thank you so much for traveling all this way, Mr. James. It means so much to me," Ben said, wiping away his tears.

"My grandfather flew to Kansas City, literally hours after I told him of your mother's passing. I'm so sorry for your loss, Ben. Thank you for letting me know," Doug Tamworth, who was next in line said after Mr. James moved along to shake Mr. Gilsum's hand and tell him how proud he should be of his son.

"Thank you for coming here, and for bringing your grandfather. It's great to see you, Doug," Ben replied.

"We wouldn't have missed it. Kansas City's only a three-hour drive. I'll bring my grandfather back, perhaps in a week or so, and we can catch up on matters related to the Brothers of Herrad. That's only if you're ready, no pressure," Doug added.

Ben just nodded. *There's not much to discuss with me about the Brothers, Doug. You wanna talk about my bake sale? My long list of members? One and counting.*

After the service ended, an incredibly long line of cars made the trip a half mile north on 1st Avenue to Hillcrest Cemetery to lay Mrs. Gilsum to rest. The scenery at Hillcrest appeared peaceful and wide open, with plenty of green.

Many of the graves were marked with flat stones, but there were about a dozen beautiful headstones on the graves around his mother's final resting place. Ben felt proud that his mother would have a headstone over her grave, something he insisted on doing for her, but he knew she wouldn't want one if there were no others at the cemetery. *This is the perfect place Mom. Great choice.*

Ben looked around the vast crowd of friends and strangers gathered around. *I knew there were a lot of people at the wake, but I had no idea there would be this many here at the funeral.*

As he scanned the crowd, his eyes locked with another familiar face from DC. A woman in her late twenties, tall, standing straight, with both arms resting at her sides. Though she wasn't wearing a uniform, she looked like a soldier, standing at attention. She gave Ben a quick nod with a respectful look on her face, acknowledging his gaze and offering her sympathies, without saying a word.

Holy shit. Is that Ms. Green?

Chapter 26

Long after the funeral service concluded, Ben sat on a bench at Hillcrest Cemetery, alone, watching the grounds crew bury his mother from a distance. The family didn't plan a gathering for after the funeral, despite Aunt Lilian's vigorous objections. Ben and his father didn't want anything to do with a large crowd of people, making small talk at the family's home, or anywhere else. Both men wanted to be alone, preferring to handle their grief in private. The thought of guests in the house, without the much more amiable Mrs. Gilsum there to entertain them, scared the hell out of the Gilsum men.

Ben was thinking about his dear friend, Mr. James, and a conversation the two had before the older man left town. Mr. James and his grandson Doug made plans with Ben to return to Arkansas to discuss the status of the Brothers of Herrad in Decatur.

"I'll be back to work next week, at John Brown University. But I'm only assisting my boss with one class till the end of this semester, then we break for winter in two weeks. I have plenty of free time at JBU during the week, if you feel comfortable meeting with me there. My evening schedule is pretty busy, I'm working hard to complete my master's program, and writing for a history journal. I'll be working around the clock over Christmas break, hoping to get the club open after the holidays. I'd prefer we meet at the university within the next two weeks," Ben told them.

"Very well, Ben. If you want we'll come and see you at JBU on Wednesday. Been a while since I've been down that way. Beautiful campus."

Great, looking forward to it. No idea what we're gonna talk about. I'm sure it'll be swell, though. Ben was drowning in an overwhelming sense of guilt for losing interest in the Brothers of Herrad after everything its founder, Mr. James, did for him. The old church building, funding for the Decatur Club for Boys and Girls. Ben could never have accomplished those things without Mr. James.

That's just half of it. Mr. James understands me. His guidance during our talks in Virginia helped make me a more confident person. He changed my life. There's just too much happening right now. I do want to run the club, that's a dream come true. But with going back to school, taking on a new job, writing a book? I just don't have the bandwidth to run a private society. Recruit members? Secure funding? I think I know what needs to be discussed between me and the Tamworths. I'm just not sure I have the guts to do it.

Lost in thought, Ben didn't notice the slender, soldier-like woman quietly sit down, just a few feet away from him, on the same metal bench, as the burial crew completed their work. She'd been watching him a while, waiting for the right moment to approach and speak with him after their eyes caught one another during the funeral service.

The staccato knocks of a red-bellied woodpecker disturbed the quiet, peaceful cemetery, and distracted Ben from his groggy trance. As his gaze drifted to the left to look for the bird he nearly jumped out of his seat at seeing the warm, brown eyes of the tall, attractive woman looking back at him. *When the hell did she get there?*

"Hello, Ben. I'm sorry to startle you. I never got a chance to talk with you at either of the services today. I wanted to tell you how deeply sorry I am for your loss."

"Thank you, Ms. Green."

"You can call me Reina now, Ben. My name is Reina Dario," she announced and slid closer, offering a handshake and a comforting pat on Ben's shoulder.

"Reina Dario? You know, I always assumed your real name was something like Athena, or Elektra. Or something badass, like that. But Reina's nice, too." Ben chuckled at himself for being such a clod.

Reina didn't respond verbally. She offered a polite smile with tilted head and raised brow instead.

He couldn't help but notice Reina wore a skirt, something he'd never seen her wear before. It seemed incredibly out of character, but the tall-athletic, former soldier wore it well.

"Why are you telling me your real name? Shouldn't I be addressing you as Ms. Green still, even though I don't work at the company anymore? Isn't it inappropriate for me to know anything personal about you?" Ben asked.

"I don't work for that department in the government anymore. I'm a field agent for the FBI. I get to bust the bad guys face to face, in person. Mix it up a little sometimes, you know? The good stuff," Reina declared, making a fist with her right hand and raising it below her chin with a scowl on her face.

"Well, they picked the right person for the job, but I have to be honest. I really liked the idea of having you behind the scenes in Federal Law Enforcement. You were a welcome upgrade over who worked there before you. I hope whoever's there now can properly fill your shoes."

Reina didn't respond to the compliment right away. She took a deep breath and gazed out at the same green scenery Ben had lost himself in before she sat down next to him.

"Well, Ben, when you shook things up in my office last year, I had some serious soul searching to do. You remember how disappointed you were when it became evident the Sullivans were walking away? Not a single charge? Not so much as an investigation? As I'm sure you remember, we weren't supposed to offer personal opinions in that line of work, but I felt it, too. I still do. It still burns me. And that file's sealed now, like we promised it would be. So, people like me can't touch any of the evidence in there or use it to bust an entire list of corporate and elected criminals. A lot of people got a free pass because of the power and influence of Bradford Sullivan. And to avoid the embarrassment of it becoming public that we had a couple bad eggs on the inside," Reina admitted.

"I knew you felt the same. You have a strong poker face, but I could sense your anger back then. I don't see it now, though. In fact, you're a heck of a lot more personable, *Reina,* than I've ever seen you before. It's nice to talk with you like this. You don't remind me of a cyborg anymore."

"Nice, Ben, thanks for that," Reina laughed.

Special Agent Dario quickly shifted the conversation away from herself and back to her experiences in DC. "Everyone involved with the Sullivans has either moved on or been shown the door. Things are better now, and my former superiors are more alert and sensitive to improper behavior. As for me, you can say I've answered my true calling. This is what I love doing. And I have you to thank for helping me discover that."

"And the list of criminals? The rest of them, that aren't Bradford Sullivan? What happens to them?" Ben couldn't help but ask.

"Well, I can't open the old file. But I'm free to keep my eyes open and pointed in the right direction in case some of our old friends do something stupid again. Some of them already have."

"Are you watching Bradford Sullivan?" Ben asked, knowing Reina wouldn't answer the question.

"Bradford Sullivan is dead. Cancer," Reina answered.

"Oh, my God. That's a shame," Ben said, respectfully.

"You know I can't tell you what I'm investigating. Let's just say I'm interested in some of our old friends, still living, and leave it at that."

"Fair enough. I have another question for you. What brings you to Arkansas? How did you know my mother died?"

"Don't worry, Ben. I'm definitely not investigating you. You're one of the good guys. The best, actually. One of our mutual contacts, a coworker of yours at the company I've kept in touch with, told me they saw a Facebook post about your mother. I wanted to be here for you, to offer support and pay respects."

Ben stared a while at Reina and smiled. It was nice talking with her, and for a moment she helped him forget the deep sorrow he felt over saying goodbye to his mother. He knew she wasn't being honest with him about how she heard of his mother's death. *She knows I know that's bullshit.*

Reina smiled back at Ben. She gave him a warm hug and a surprise kiss on the cheek, before getting up and walking away.

What the heck is Ms. Green, or Reina Dario, doing in Arkansas? She's acting like a completely different person. I'm also pretty sure she knows I've never had a Facebook account.

Chapter 27

It took a couple nights in his own bed before Ben woke up feeling ready for the day. He'd spent the rest of the week after the funeral sleeping at his father's house. The young man went back to his apartment Sunday night, declaring he needed some sleep if he expected to make it to work on Monday. By Wednesday morning the effects of sleeping on the short-lumpy couch were sufficiently worn away.

As usual, Ben tried to sort out life during the drive to work. "I can't figure out how I feel about Aunt Lillian living with Dad at the house, alone. They're either gonna kill each other or end up married."

The thought of his father living alone with another woman, even a relative, didn't sit well at all with Ben. He knew there was nothing to worry about, at least for now. His father loved his mother deeply. They had never left that to doubt, and it was confirmed by the visible pain Mr. Gilsum had exhibited since hearing the doctor say he was sorry.

"I'm gonna have to keep an eye on those two," Ben laughed at himself. "Not that I could do anything to stop them if they decided to not hate each other anymore. I wonder if all of that was just an act. Overcompensate much? Ugh. What am I doing? I don't even wanna think about it."

The reluctant Worshipful Master forced himself to shift his thoughts to a more pressing matter. "Mr. James and Doug Tamworth are meeting me for lunch today, to talk about the Brothers of Herrad."

Ben looked at the leather-bound book on the passenger seat. The book stayed with the Worshipful Master of the Brothers and contained information about every lodge in the organization, as well as the secret writings of Herrad of Landsburg, which provided the inspiration Mr. James had used to start the group fifty years ago. The gold ring, with the letter *M* on the bezel was on top of the book, and not on the current Worshipful Master's finger, where it was supposed to be.

"I still don't know how I'm gonna tell them. Maybe it won't be so hard. Doug already knows about the bake sale, and he did not seem pleased. I had to tell him I had *some* plans. The turnout was nice, and we'll get the Community Room painted. But not one new member. And not a penny of funding for anything else. Not to mention, no future plans."

Ben's thoughts shifted to the one thing that still mattered to him about the Brothers of Herrad; his mentor. The two had developed a special bond during Ben's training for initiation into the group. Mr. James insisted he be the one to work with Ben, though he hadn't mentored an initiate since before the young man's birth. He felt excited about the opportunity after discovering Ben's unique qualities and talent.

They had spent several Sundays, talking for hours. The first half of each session was devoted to learning about the Brothers of Herrad, and during the second half they talked about something Mr. James knew the two had in common. Mr. James understood the social struggles Ben faced because of his extremely introverted personality combined with his high degree of empathy.

Talking with his mentor about his personality and character traits helped Ben to better understand why he behaved the way he did, why he avoided contact with other people and why he had lived inside an impenetrable shell for most of his life. The young man learned that being guarded from the anger and sadness in the world around him also meant he created a barrier to the joy and love. Those conversations with Mr. James had improved Ben's life immeasurably.

Not yet having an assigned parking space of his own at JBU, Ben searched for a spot in the employee parking lot. A heavy sigh escaped his lips as he slid the Jeep into park and turned off the engine. "I hate this. I don't know if I'm doing the right thing. I do know Mr. James deserves someone who will give his organization more time and effort. I'm not that person."

Ben lifted the leather-bound book and ring from his passenger seat, placed them in his messenger bag and made his way to his office.

"I really don't want to disappoint Mr. James."

Chapter 28

Doug Tamworth laughed at the question his grandfather asked as he looked at him through the rearview mirror of his brown Lexus LS 500. The ninety-nine-year-old found it much easier to get in, and especially out of the back seat of his grandson's car. Mr. James was confused about the venue chosen for their lunch meeting with Ben.

"Honestly, Grandad, I don't know what a Ziggywurst is either. We don't have any of those in Missouri. I'm pretty sure this place isn't part of a franchise. And if it is, I've never heard of it. It's just the name of a German restaurant in Siloam Springs. That's where Ben wants us to meet him for lunch. I didn't pick it."

Mr. James laughed. "I'm sure if Ben picked it, it'll be perfect."

Doug didn't respond, except with a shake of his head that his grandfather didn't notice.

"I'm worried about him, Doug. Not just because he lost his mother, that's a pain that softens in due time. Maybe I'm more worried about us, because we may be losing him. After all that's happened these last two years, he stuck with us. I feel as though he's slipping away now, even with getting his life back on track and finding his true calling at the university. I think it's only a matter of time before he resigns," Mr. James predicted.

"I'm starting to believe that may be better for all of us, including him," Doug replied, pouncing on the opportunity to tell his grandfather his thoughts on the topic.

Mr. James didn't respond. He had sensed Doug's resentment over Ben's ascension to Worshipful Master, a role he knew his grandson coveted. Mr. James still didn't believe his grandson would be the Worshipful Master he envisioned for the Brothers of Herrad.

"Grandad, he's made excellent progress in all aspects of his new life back in Arkansas. He's found the right career, and he's working hard to pursue that. He's only about a month away from opening a successful club for underprivileged children. The whole town is behind him on it. The man has shown us how hard he works when his heart is with something. Which brings me to my point. He's done absolutely nothing about the Brothers of Herrad in the months since accepting the ring."

"I wouldn't call what happened recently down there nothing, Douglas."

"Are you referring to the bake sale? He raised three hundred dollars putting on a bake sale. You're right. I suppose that's not *nothing*."

"It's not the money that matters, it's the response from the community. They loved it. Half the town showed up. People are still taking about the plans to paint the Community Center. This type of community activity is worth far more than money. This is exactly what I had in mind when I started the Brothers of Herrad, and I fear Ben may be the only person who gets it." Mr. James was adamant about that last point.

"Well, don't be so sure he gets it. He seemed awfully embarrassed by the bake sale when he told me all the details. I think he considers the event a failure just as much as I do." Doug waited briefly for a response. "Grandad, I don't think Ben's heart is in it right now. I know you think he's special. I agree with you. He's a great kid. I don't know a more honorable man. I just think he's in over his head."

"He has a lot on his plate right now," Mr. James said, defending his friend.

"You know what else? He has no clue that today is the first Wednesday of December. It never occurred to him that today was the most appropriate day for us to meet, because the Brothers of Herrad always meet on the first Wednesday of the month for Assembly. It was the first thing I thought about when we made plans to meet today."

Mr. James had nothing further to say to his grandson. He felt upset with himself for emboldening Doug the way he did, opening the door for all the criticism of Ben. The old man sat silently for a few moments, determining it would be best to think before speaking again. He let out a sigh and gazed at the wheat fields flying by. *Ben, don't give up on us yet. We've only just begun. There's so much more we can accomplish together.*

Chapter 29

Ben waved at Mr. James and Doug when they entered Ziggywurst. He smiled as they approached, though he dreaded this meeting. Ben knew what he had to say would not be taken well, but he felt excited to see his old friend. Their last communication, prior to his mother's funeral, was a letter Mr. James left in an empty Brothers of Herrad lodge in Alexandria, Virginia, apologizing for not being there in person to inform him the lodge was disbanded, due to the illicit behavior of its leaders, Bradford and William Sullivan. Ben had no idea if he would ever see Mr. James again, or if the letter signified the end of his membership with the organization. The letter included a promise that a close associate would provide Ben with further detail about his future with the group. It wasn't until several months later, in Decatur that Ben realized he'd been chosen by Mr. James to be the next Worshipful Master of the Brothers.

Ben couldn't help but laugh when he noticed Mr. James wore his customary wool slacks with sneakers, and a sweater over a dress shirt. No tie. He'd seen him in this outfit at least two dozen times when they met in DC, and again at his mother's funeral.

"Mr. James, it's so nice to see you. Thanks again for being there last week."

"Wouldn't have missed it, Ben. Tell me, Son, when will you ever just call me Jim?" Mr. James asked.

"Old habits die hard, Mr. James, like your wardrobe choice. I'll tell you what, I'll call you Jim when you change your style." Ben smiled, poking fun at his beloved friend.

"What's wrong with my wardrobe? I wear the same style of clothing every day for a perfectly functional reason. This way I never have to waste time thinking about what to wear. That, my friend, is a trick I learned from Albert Einstein. So it must have merit."

Ben smiled wider and shrugged in agreement, gave Doug a welcoming handshake, and the trio sat down to look at a menu. *Don't ask me the difference between a wurst and a schnitzel. I still don't know.*

"Ben, I'm so pleased you've begun a teaching career at the university. Not many of us are blessed with the opportunity to follow our true calling. I believe you've found yours," Mr. James said, starting the conversation.

"I have to admit, I'm extremely fortunate they even considered me for the job. I don't have the resume of a typical Assistant Professor. Lucky for me the department head knew me well, or I'd still be a cost estimator at the plant. Come to think of it, I don't have the resume for that job either," Ben chuckled wryly.

"Well that should tell you something about yourself that I know you're uncomfortable admitting. You can do *anything* you try. Your department head at JBU was wise enough to figure that out and take a chance on you, and so were the folks at the plant," Mr. James speculated, knowing his star pupil never liked receiving compliments.

"How are things going with the Decatur Club for Boys and Girls?" Doug asked, changing the subject.

"I'm still waiting for a few pieces of equipment for the playground and the final approval from the town. But I expect we'll open our doors sometime next month. We're on schedule," Ben announced.

"That's great, Ben. We're really proud of what you're doing there," Mr. James said as their order came to the table.

Ben and Mr. James exchanged small talk while they ate. Doug remained quiet the entire time. Ben experienced a feeling of dread, knowing only one topic remained uncovered.

Doug seems more fidgety than I remember. He's anxious. Why is he so nervous? I'm the only one here who should be nervous.

After lunch was cleared away, they settled down again to have the conversation Ben didn't want to have.

"Well, Brother Gilsum, do you know what today is?" Doug asked.

"Um, Wednesday?"

"Yes, Ben, it's Wednesday. It's also the first Wednesday of December. As you know, the Brothers assemble on the first

Wednesday of every month," Doug announced, shooting a victorious look at his grandfather.

"Right. I did know that. Sorry, I've been so busy with the club and work at JBU, also going to class for my masters. I didn't really think about that," the Worshipful Master admitted.

"Well, I did hear report of an event in your hometown, sponsored by the Brothers. A very successful event, in fact, attended by half the town. You've managed to raise funds to paint the Community Center, if I'm not mistaken," Mr. James added.

"You mean the bake sale?" Doug made no effort to mask his discontent.

"Right, that. We didn't exactly fill the coffers with that one, and it's just one room at the Community Center we're having painted. The whole town uses it for meetings and assemblies. It's kind of important to Decatur."

Mr. James shot an angered look back at his grandson.

"My philosophy on community events has always been that a heavy involvement is far more valuable than heavy donations. From what I heard, I'd say the event was a huge success. Don't be concerned about the money," Mr. James insisted.

Mr. James looked at Doug again and continued. "Besides, gentlemen, concern about money is exactly what nearly destroyed our entire organization when the Sullivans were at the helm. Don't ever forget that."

Doug didn't respond. His expression remained unchanged. It became more obvious that Doug felt disappointed with the current direction of the Brothers. *He's gonna make this easy for me.*

"Ben, do you remember your training? I told you all we can ever hope to accomplish as we do our good deeds, is that people will recognize them. And hopefully follow our example. You can't buy righteousness. No amount of money will ever prove humanity worthy of enlightenment. Money actually has a history of proving otherwise."

Recognizing the shot fired at Doug Tamworth made Ben remember something both Doug and Billy Sullivan had said to him about his involvement with the Brothers of Herrad. "Relax, you're a part of something special." *It doesn't feel very special anymore.*

For the first time, Ben had no confusion about what he wanted to do. The only thing special about the Brothers of Herrad sat to his right wearing wool pants with sneakers. The time had come for Ben to take control of the conversation. And now it wouldn't be so hard.

"Mr. James, Doug, there's no point in discussing this any further. I've made a decision. My life has changed since coming back to Arkansas. While I intend to keep working hard for the community and volunteering both time and money, I don't believe anymore that I need to be part of a larger organization to accomplish that. I just want to be a good man, a good teacher, a good coach and mentor to a handful of kids who can really use one. Right now, that's plenty good enough for me," Ben said, stopping when he saw the ever-present smile on Mr. James face disappear.

"Are you certain this is what you want, Son?" Mr. James asked.

"I've given it a great deal of thought. I'm certain. Teaching at the university and mentoring at the club are going to take all my time, and then some. You deserve to have someone in charge of the Brothers who can give you more," Ben answered as he pulled the leather-bound book and gold ring with the letter *M* on the bezel out of his messenger bag and slid them across the table toward Doug.

Ben noticed a faint smile creeping up on Doug's face that he couldn't hide. *I knew you'd like that Doug. You've wanted these items to be yours since long before we met, didn't you?*

"If you want me to return the money you donated to the club, I will. I can survive on donations. And my salary at JBU will cover the rest. We'll get by. I hope you and I can remain friends, Jim. I love you like a father and this doesn't change that."

"That donation was a gift, not a condition. Same goes for the old church. The building and funding are yours to do with as you see fit. You don't owe us anything, Son. Thank you for your honesty and your friendship. I'd very much like for us to keep in touch and remain friends. You're a special young man, Ben. I'm better for knowing you," Mr. James' voice was shaking.

Doug appeared pleased for the first time during the lunch meeting. He gave Ben a stern handshake and wished him good luck.

Ben didn't speak to Doug. *There's still something off about him. Like he knows something I don't know. Maybe he's just excited to finally get what he wants.*

Mr. James stood up. He gave Doug a look and pointed toward the door, indicating to his grandson that it was time to go.

Ben watched as the two got into Doug's car and waved at Mr. James as they drove away.

I wonder if I'll ever see either of them again.

On the road back to Kansas City, Doug stared at the leather-bound book and ring that now rested on the passenger seat of his car and smiled. He looked in the rear-view mirror to check on his grandfather.

"Don't worry, Grandad. Everything's going to work out fine," he declared.

"Oh, I'm sure it will. It always does. I can't help but think to myself, we should have never taken Ben away from Arkansas."

Chapter 30

Spending Thursday after work with Miranda Swanzey proved to be exactly what Ben needed. He'd been wrestling with guilt about saying goodbye to the Brothers and Mr. James the day before. The two drove to an art shop in Gravette together to buy acrylic paint, brushes, and other supplies to start the mural in the Community Room. They circled back to Lowes in Siloam Springs to get the rest of the necessary supplies. Miranda invited Ben to join her for a drink at her favorite spot in town, Creekside Taproom.

Ben felt completely at ease with Miranda, like they were friends for years, even though they'd only met a few weeks earlier. The differences in their personalities seemed to work in their favor, and Ben couldn't imagine anyone not getting along well with her. She had a warm, accepting nature. She listened to Ben when he told her about his worries and concerns, never telling him what he was doing wrong, or trying to fix him. In return, Ben offered a special kindness to Miranda that she'd grown to appreciate dearly. He clearly needed a friend, and he clearly valued her friendship. He was open and honest, and never expected anything in return for his kindness.

Creekside Taproom appealed to Ben immediately. The old industrial-historic building with exposed brick and steel reminded him a little of his favorite spot in Alexandria, The Columbia Firehouse. The owners, a local couple, kept the bar well stocked with draft beer made from Arkansas-based craft breweries and created a fantastic environment for locals to feel welcome, along with occasional visitors from out of town.

I can see this being my regular Thursday spot, after work.

"You seem like you're in a better mood today than I've noticed in weeks. What's up with you today?" Miranda asked from across their table near the bar.

"I am in a good mood. A really good mood," Ben admitted.

"Yeah? That's great. You gonna tell me why, or you gonna just keep looking at me with that goofy smile on your face?"

"You know how I was having a hard time trying to figure out how to get people to sign up for the Brothers of Herrad? Totally stressing out about it?" Ben asked.

"Ah, yes. The mysterious secret society no one's ever heard of. I remember," Miranda answered.

"Private society. And yesterday, I quit. I handed back the ring you asked me about," Ben said, holding up his right hand to show there was nothing on his ring finger.

"Good for you. You don't strike me as the type to be involved with some shady secret society anyway. I don't trust them. Or any other secret society for that matter," Miranda declared.

"Private society. Most people think they're all bad, but they do a lot of really great things for the community. They raise millions of dollars to help with children's charities all over the country."

"I have a question for you darlin'. Was your *private society* bad?" Miranda asked.

"Um. Well. If I'm being completely honest, yeah. At times they were bad. At times they were very bad," Ben answered.

"Hmm. Welcome back to the world of the innocent, my friend. It's good to have you back," Miranda said, lifting her beer glass for a toast.

The bartender approached the table with two fresh beers that neither Ben nor Miranda asked for, "These are on the house, you two. The owners asked me to bring a drink to the lovely couple before you ordered a second round."

Miranda thanked the bartender and nodded to the owners of the bar to show her appreciation.

Ben laughed. "The lovely couple?"

"Eh, just go with it. It's a free beer."

Ben just smiled and gave a thank you nod to the owners.

"Don't you get any ideas, Mr. Gilsum. You told me all about Patty, who was perfect by the way, and how excited you were to see her. Then you dropped her like a hot stone when she finally came out here for a visit. Your heart and mind belong to someone else, whether you realize it or not. And it sure isn't me. Besides, we work together. *And* we'll be spending time volunteering together at the club, and we have a pretty great friendship brewing. I don't want you screwing any of that up." Miranda's sharp wit was endearing.

"Did you just friend zone me?" Ben asked, laughing.

"Damn straight, buddy. Consider yourself locked in."

Ben laughed again and sipped his beer, compliments of the house. *My heart belongs to someone else? Has she been talking to my parents? Or is it just that obvious to anyone who knows me?*

Chapter 31

John Brown University emptied rapidly as students were packing up and returning home for winter break. Ben and Dr. Orchard finished grading finals to post grades for students before going off to celebrate the holidays with their families. Ben had one more meeting with his boss about his history journal submission before he could work on the finishing touches. Whatever time remained during the break would be used to finalize the syllabus for his first class as a professor in the spring, HST 2113 United States History to 1865. He'd also have to squeeze in some time to prepare the Decatur Club for Boys and Girls for its opening day in January.

"I've read all of your notes and drafts, and I have to say this is good stuff. I enjoyed reading the wealth of information about Dr. Joseph Warren, and I like your list of founding fathers who were Freemasons," Dr. Orchard declared. "Nine of the Declaration's fifty six signers? I honestly thought there were more, but it's the names you mention that are striking. I didn't know about John Hancock. Don't tell anyone I admitted that."

"I'm sworn to secrecy, Dr. Orchard," Ben smirked.

"Your theories of how Freemasonry had *some* influence during the formation of our nation are solid. I'm pleased that you relaxed the amount of influence from your previous draft. Too much speculation is dangerous."

Ben nodded. *I still believe my original notes were accurate, but, oh, well.*

"The mention of Freemason symbols scattered all over the capital are OK, but don't take that any further. Remember, your focus is on Dr. Warren. The readers won't mind straying off topic a little. I didn't. But don't go too far."

Ben nodded. *I don't believe I went far enough.*

"In my opinion, none of what you've written is over the top. You avoided fantasy and conspiracy rather nicely. Most of this stuff is generally accepted, and you offered a few new ideas that aren't hard to consider. I like the stuff about Dr. Warren being a top option, but not a lock, as our nation's first president had he survived the Revolution. I find it hard to believe anyone could have beaten out George Washington for that honor," Dr. Orchard added.

Ben smiled, but knew he wasn't out of the woods yet. Dr. Orchard tended to list all the positives ahead of the negatives. And though the assistant professor pulled the speculation back considerably on his latest draft, there were still points he refused to back away from. *OK, I'm bracing myself. I'm ready for the "but".*

"Now, about your insistence that Benedict Arnold may have remained loyal to the United States had Dr. Warren survived. Are you sure I can't talk you off that cliff? You're humanizing the most noteworthy traitor in American History. Benedict Arnold is perhaps the United States' first villain. You don't need to defend that man in order to get your paper published," Dr. Orchard pleaded.

"Everything we read in history books tells us my theory is wrong. Benedict Arnold was riddled with debt, surrounded by scandal, and married to a woman whose family were loyalists. But he was never indicted for any of those scandals. There was no evidence. The facts around the trials suggest most of it may have been political. And his military superiors, particularly George Washington, always spoke highly of him. All the way to the end. I've read his letters, and I can sense how troubled he felt. The conflict he faced." *I've compromised enough. This is still my article.*

"That conflict was common among many of the founding fathers. Benedict Arnold was not the only one who risked it all. He was certainly not the only one who considered switching sides in order to save his hide, or his fortune. Those risks are what immortalized our founding fathers. They most certainly don't excuse Benedict Arnold for being a traitor," Dr. Orchard replied.

"I agree completely, Dr. Orchard. The incredible risks and sacrifices made by our founding fathers, and every American soldier since the Revolutionary War, are not just part of lore. They're real, and the people who took them and continue to take them, without wavering should be honored and celebrated.

Those hardships should never be used as an excuse to turn traitor. That's definitely not my intention. I'm only suggesting he didn't come to the decision to turn easily. He could have been persuaded, by the right person, to remain loyal."

"Very well. I've another question. I couldn't find any connection between Dr. Warren and Benedict Arnold. How were you able to find these letters you've mentioned?" Dr. Orchard asked.

"Most of their communication is documented in Freemason archives," Ben answered.

"Secret societies? Well, I don't need to remind you about my feelings of such organizations. And I'm not alone there. I hope your involvement with, what do they call themselves again, the Brothers of Herrad? I hope your involvement with that group isn't influencing your understanding of American History," Dr. Orchard warned.

"I've left the Brothers of Herrad to focus on my teaching career, among other personal pursuits. They have no influence over me whatsoever."

"That's a relief. Well done, Mr. Gilsum. Back to your paper then. You could be facing an incredible amount of push back. Or worse, you could be ignored completely. Nothing you've said to me about Benedict Arnold suggests anything but an opinion."

"I'll admit that. I'll make it clear that this is only a theory based on interpretation of letters and accounts. I don't mean to present any of this as fact. Besides, this theory is only a small part of my paper." The hair was up on the back of Ben's neck.

"Sometimes, my friend, we see something so clearly because we want to so badly. Not because it's actually there. That's why, as historians we must always rely exclusively on accepted fact. Not to mention, even if this particular theory of yours is presented as a single paragraph in a fifty-thousand word manuscript, someone is going to magnify it and use it to judge the entire document. They'll call you a hack and question your talent. It's a risk, but it's yours to take," Dr. Orchard offered.

"I want to take that risk. I'll include every letter, every account of conversation, everything I have that makes me believe my idea *could* be true. I understand why people will think I'm nuts, but I'm not just pulling this idea out of the air. There's documentation that at least suggests it's possible. Before turning, Benedict Arnold was a true patriot. Had he remained loyal, he'd have been a hero, that's what made his turning so notorious. That's why it came as such a shock to his peers. It's not my belief in Benedict Arnold that leads me to what I'm suggesting. It's my strong belief in the man that Dr. Joseph Warren was. And that's what my article is all about."

Dr. Orchard dropped his head and let out a labored sigh. "I admire your passion. Witnessing such passion in youth is what I enjoy most about teaching. My job, my promise is to present students with as much fact as I can and then get the hell out of the way while they form their own opinions. I refuse to violate that promise. I've offered you all the advice I can." He did his best to hide his disappointment. "Enjoy the winter break. Write your paper, include the facts, and offer your theories. Fill it with your passion. What will be will be."

Chapter 32

Angelina Rindge was staring at the untouched White Zinfandel Sangria Lemonade her mother insisted she try. She was alone at her father's reserved table at the Boston Yacht Club in Marblehead, Massachusetts. She wore a pink dress at her mother's request that she swore she'd burn after the event, in honor of the fundraiser for the Breast Cancer Foundation. Her father attended many such fundraisers at the Yacht Club, usually as a special guest of some influential friend, and the entire family would come to help him impress them. Angelina typically stayed at her father's side to socialize with his powerful friends. Her beauty and charm made Robert much more appealing to them. This time, however, the third-year law student, home for winter break, wasn't in the mood.

The beautiful harbor-side hotel was founded in 1866 and its yacht club members included several America's Cup champions over its one hundred and fifty year history. The Main Lounge was used for private functions and could accommodate about fifty to one hundred very wealthy individuals.

Angelina looked at her vibrating cellphone with disgust. She nearly put it back in her Bottega Veneta top handle bag but remembered what Special Agent Dario asked her to do when Billy Sullivan called: "Answer the call…Get him to talk about Ben…Write down everything he says."

She quickly made her way outside the dining room where cell phone use was strictly prohibited by club rules.

"Hello, Billy. Please tell me you're calling from Southie, or some other place that's nowhere near Arkansas," Angelina answered.

"Two answered calls in a row? Damn. If I didn't know any better, I'd believe you were sweet on me again, Angel," Billy declared.

"Cut the shit, Billy. Where are you?"

"I'm sorry to disappoint you, *again,* but I'm still in Kansas City. But don't worry, beautiful, I'll be home in no time at all. My plan's in motion. I have everything I need now, with the help of some heavy hitters. It's amazing what these guys can come up with. I'm just waiting for the perfect time to strike."

"Billy, I told you I didn't want you to go after Ben. I made it pretty clear when I said if you did, I'd want nothing to do with you. You're gonna get caught. You'll go to prison for the rest of your life or get yourself killed."

"That's what you said, I do remember. You also said you were worried about *me*. Well don't worry so much. This plan is perfect. I won't get caught, thanks to the help of my friends in high places. It'll all work out perfectly. I'll be seeing you soon, Angel. I promise."

Angelina wanted to threaten Billy or warn him that she'd call the cops. She thought about telling him she already spoke to the FBI, and they were probably listening to the call right now. But she remembered Agent Dario and decided to try and get as much information as she could from him instead. *He's already shown me he's dumb enough to tell me what he's doing. I bet I can find out when and how too.*

"When are you gonna do it, Billy? What day?"

"Well, they already had one death in the family. The little rat's mother just died. Maybe I'll give them some time to mourn her before they lose another," Billy said with an inhumane chuckle.

"His mother died?" Angelina asked, forgetting to pretend she didn't care about Ben.

"Yeah, the old lady's been sick forever. She finally kicked a little more than a week ago. I hope he's hurting. He's definitely a momma's boy."

Angelina fought her desire to tell Billy what she thought of him and persisted, "When are you going after him Billy?"

Billy didn't answer, and for a while the line went silent.

"Billy, are you there? Tell me what you're up to. I need to know when to expect you. We can make plans now if you want."

Billy thought again for a moment, keeping the line silent.

"I think we have a bad connection, Angel. You're breaking up pretty badly. Tell you what, I'll call you when I'm heading back to Boston. I can't wait to see you again. Bye for now, beautiful girl," Billy added before he hung up the perfectly clear line.

Chapter 33

Angelina quickly realized she didn't have Reina Dario's card in the hand bag she'd taken with her to the Boston Yacht Club. *Why didn't I just add her to my contact list? I need to go. I need to go now.*

"Mom, I can't find Dad. Tell him I took an Uber home. Something's come up and I need to get home, now."

Mrs. Rindge tried to speak, but Angelina interrupted her.

"No, wait. He'll worry. Just tell him I wasn't feeling well. No big deal, just wanted to go home and get some rest," Angelina told her mother.

"Are you OK, sweetie? What's going on? I can call Marta and ask her to come get you if you're not feeling well," Mrs. Rindge offered.

"Everything's fine. I'm fine. I need to make an emergency phone call. A friend is in trouble. I can't wait for Marta to drive out here and get me. I already called Uber and the driver's gonna be here any minute."

"Emergency? If everything's fine, what's the emergency?" Mrs. Rindge asked.

"Not me. A friend. I promise, Mom. I'm fine. Tell Daddy for me, please. And don't tell him I was freaked out or anything. There's nothing to worry about," Angelina insisted.

"You're telling me not to worry, but you're acting a little crazy right now. If you want me to relax, I need you to calm down and explain to me what's going on."

"I'm gonna be taking a trip. To visit a friend in Arkansas. I'll be home before Christmas. Maybe. I dunno. I need to go, now."

"Arkansas?" Mrs. Rindge stopped a moment to think. "Isn't Ben from Arkansas?"

Angelina didn't answer and ran out the door as her mother stood there watching in confusion, unable to stop her.

After a forty minute Uber ride home, Angelina rushed into her parents' house, kicked off her heels and ran to her bedroom, flying past a confused Marta.

She found Agent Dario's card in her wallet and dialed while booting up her laptop to find the earliest flight from Boston to somewhere near Decatur, Arkansas.

"Miss Rindge, what have you got to tell me?" Agent Dario asked, knowing there must have been a development if Angelina Rindge dialed her number.

"Billy called me. He's going after Ben, soon. He wouldn't tell me when, but it's gonna happen any day now, I know it. Someone needs to stop him. Now!"

"Miss Rindge, I need you to calm down, right now. I'm in Decatur. I've been watching Billy Sullivan's every move. If he moves toward Ben, I'll be on him. I promise."

"I'm coming down there. I need to see Ben. I need to be there for him," Angelina declared.

"Miss Rindge, don't do that. Don't lose control. Think about what you're doing. If Billy finds out you're down here, he could get spooked. You also have to consider your own safety. I can't allow you to take that risk."

"Can you stop me?"

"Yes, Angel. I can stop you," Agent Dario answered sternly.

"Well, you're gonna have to shoot me, Special Agent Dario. I'm going to see Ben. I'm on the next flight to, I don't fucking know where. Northwest Arkansas Regional, wherever the hell that is," Angelina said, and turned off her cellphone.

Chapter 34

Reina Dario waited alone, inside the TSA security screening point, at the gate while Angelina and fellow passengers walked off the plane at Norwest Arkansas Regional. She stood tall, with perfect posture, staring straight ahead, like a Marine Guard standing at attention with her hands at her sides. She hardly moved until she saw Angelina Rindge walking out of the gangway, heading toward her.

"Miss Rindge. I hope you had a comfortable flight. I assume you had time to rationalize your next move," Agent Dario said as she walked with Angelina, who had only brought carry-on luggage, toward the terminal exit.

"I suppose I shouldn't bother asking you how you knew which flight I was on. Or how you got into the gate area without a boarding pass."

"I suppose you shouldn't, Miss Rindge," Agent Dario answered, softening her tone.

She tried to present a friendly demeanor, but Reina Dario almost always looked like a soldier on a dangerous mission, no matter what she was doing. She appeared both beautiful and intimidating to most people. Angelina felt completely at awe of her and frightened by her.

"Are you here to arrest me?" Angelina asked, calmly.

"No, Angel. I'm not here to arrest you."

Angelina stopped walking toward the exit and moved toward an empty gate, motioning to Agent Dario that she'd like to have a seat and talk.

"I thought you were watching Billy. Who's watching him?" Angelina asked

"He's in Kansas City right now. That's two hundred and thirteen miles north of Ben's current location. If he moves toward Ben, I'll know it. And I'll be there in plenty of time."

"Agent Dario, I'm sorry for the way I acted on the phone yesterday. I'm not here to screw things up. I'll cooperate," Angelina offered.

"Please, Angel, call me Reina. You don't need to apologize. I feel the same emotions you're experiencing. At least to some degree. I've been trained to suppress them. Experience dealing with dangerous situations helps a person maintain a certain level of restraint. Until action becomes appropriate. Believe me, Angel, when the time comes, I intend to take appropriate action. I won't leave Ben out there alone."

"What am I supposed to do now?" Angelina asked, embarrassed by her rash behavior.

"I'm glad you asked. That's why I came here to meet you. I'd like to make you an offer, in return for your cooperation. If you'll agree to stay away from Ben and Billy, at least for now, I'll allow you to stay by my side. Safety permitting, of course. You'll know everything I know."

"I'm not sure whether you're offering me special treatment, or if you just wanna babysit me while I'm here," Angelina said sharply.

"Both, Angel. I'm not gonna lie to you. I understand your feelings toward Ben. He's my friend, too. He's a great person, worth taking a risk for. I'd never make this type of offer to someone I didn't believe deserved it. You might even learn a few things. I understand you're considering going into law enforcement after law school. I could offer you a few pointers, if you'll trust me. Based on what I've learned about you, I think you may find law enforcement to be your true calling."

"OK, *Reina*. I'm with you. I'm not really sure if I have another choice, so let's do this," Angelina relented.

"I have a feeling you're gonna be pleased with your decision," Agent Dario said as the two made their way out of the airport. *That's too bad. I kinda wanted to calm her down with a little more force. Just a little.*

Angelina dutifully followed Agent Dario to her car, parked in the "Emergency Vehicles Only" section, just outside the terminal. *I love this woman. What a badass. She might be my hero.*

Chapter 35

The University of Arkansas, in Fayetteville, was Ben's school of choice to complete the work needed for his master's degree. The program normally took two years to complete, but Ben planned to finish up in three semesters, or perhaps two if he could handle the extra work. Fayetteville is about forty miles southeast of Decatur, and Ben made the trip three times a week to attend classes. His schedule became hectic at times, but Ben didn't mind. He loved being in a classroom, whether teaching or learning.

The young standout made an impression during his first semester and started at a pace that made completion in two semesters more likely. His knowledge and passion caught the attention of Dr. Franklin Hinsdale, who had taught history at the university for thirty years after starting his career in Boston. The well-known and respected history professor had considerable influence among his peers and history departments all over the country. A Franklin Hinsdale recommendation could open doors for any aspiring professor.

Dr. Hinsdale wore a straw hat, with a wide-leather band around the crown. He almost always had a dark-brown, wooden pipe in his mouth that he chewed on more often than he smoked from. He had a full head of gray hair under his straw hat, wore glasses, and had a full-gray, neatly-trimmed beard on his face. Ben liked him instantly.

The two men shared the same passion for early American history and both specialized in the Revolutionary War. They talked about the subject for hours, during and after class.

Dr. Hinsdale surprised Ben on the last day of class before winter break by asking him for his phone number. Ben hesitated, not sure why he wanted it.

"Mr. Gilsum, I'm sorry for not first explaining my intentions. An old friend of mine at Tufts University in Boston has become aware of a remarkable and rising young talent in our field. He's become aware because I've told him all about you," Dr. Hinsdale admitted with a wink.

"Tufts? Isn't that a medical school?" Ben asked.

"They're known for their medical school, but they have a fantastic history department. They also encourage both students and professors to use their knowledge of history to theorize how people came to decisions and how events shaped ideology. They love new ideas, based on historical fact, of course. Someone like you could thrive there."

"But I already have a job at John Brown as an Assistant Professor. You know that, Dr. Hinsdale. I'm pretty lucky to be there, actually," Ben added.

"Mr. Gilsum, we're both very fortunate to be in an occupation we love, that's true. But John Brown University is lucky to have you. Don't ever doubt that."

As usual, Ben didn't respond to the compliment.

"I think you should have a conversation with my colleague in Boston. That's all. Just a conversation. I believe the two of you would hit it off. And I believe a young man who has a passion like yours for early American history should spend some time in Boston, where it all began," Dr. Hinsdale added.

Ben's mind raced as he considered the proposition. *I did fall in love with Boston when we went to see Angel's parents. And Dr. Hinsdale really liked my theory about Benedict Arnold and Dr. Joseph Warren. Is that what this is about?*

As much as I respect Dr. Orchard, he's not exactly encouraging any new ideas. But he gave me a shot that I doubt anyone else would have. I don't think I can leave JBU. And Boston? Angel's hometown? Is that a good idea?

"I'll tell you what, Mr. Gilsum. You consider it a while longer. You know how to reach me if you decide you'd like to talk to my friend at Tufts. Just a conversation."

Chapter 36

Special Agent Reina Dario looked over the perimeter of the old church building before knocking on the door. Even with Billy Sullivan over two hundred miles away in Kansas City, she wanted to scan the area and get a solid feel for the terrain. The more knowledge she had about the surroundings, the better.

The primary purpose of this visit had nothing to do with reconnaissance, however. Agent Dario felt the time had come to inform Ben of the threat to his safety. Billy's next move seemed imminent, and she wanted to be completely prepared. In order to do so, she needed Ben to be aware and focused.

"Ms. Green? I'm sorry, I mean Reina. You're still in Decatur. What are you doing here?"

"Ben, would you mind if I came inside? We need to have a conversation."

Ben invited his unexpected guest inside and motioned for her to have a seat at one of the tables in the art room.

Agent Dario looked around the room before speaking. She looked to be scanning for surveillance devices, but without the use of any special equipment that seemed impossible. Still, he didn't speak until she appeared ready. *What the hell is she looking for?*

"So, Reina, welcome to the Decatur Club for Boys and Girls," Ben said politely.

"I love what you've done with the place," Reina smiled. "But I'm afraid you may need to delay your opening."

"Delay? What for? Why are you still in town?" Ben persisted.

"Ben, I have a confession to make. I didn't find out about your mother's funeral from a Facebook post."

"Yeah, I knew that. And I'm pretty sure you know I don't even have a Facebook account," Ben speculated.

"Right. But you were too polite to mention that before. You know, one of these days someone may try to take advantage of you for being so nice," Agent Dario said with a grin. She kept walking around the room, as if she were looking for something.

"That's another thing I'm pretty sure you know. Someone already has taken advantage of me for being nice."

"Right again, Professor Gilsum."

"Assistant Professor. But someday, hopefully," Ben added.

"Ben, you're in danger," Agent Dario declared, getting to the point.

Ben didn't respond. He waited for Agent Dario to elaborate.

"You remember at the cemetery, when I told you I've been watching some of our old friends, waiting for them to do something stupid?"

Ben nodded.

"Well, it should come as no surprise at all, one of our best friends, Billy Sullivan, has done a few really stupid things. He's been watching you closely for the past several months. He's the reason I came down here. He's been here, at this building, more than once. I have reason to believe he's going to attempt to kill you."

"What?! Reason to believe?! Why didn't someone tell me this months ago?! I'm a sitting duck out here! So he's the one who's been creeping around the property in the middle of the night? How long has this maniac been stalking me?" Ben felt frantic but did his best to appear calm.

Agent Dario didn't answer. She knew Ben wasn't finished talking, so she waited for him to process what she said before responding.

"You know, I saw his car? I knew it was his car! I've seen it a couple times, but I thought I was just losing my mind. Of course it was his car. There aren't too many ninety thousand dollar cars out here in Decatur. I can't believe someone didn't tell me sooner that he's been watching me," Ben repeated with a touch of uncharacteristic anger.

Agent Dario got the sense Ben's rant was over. "Billy Sullivan is currently in Kansas City. He and his father went there after being exposed as criminals by you and your former boss, Ted Seneca. Apparently, they maintained contact with a high-ranking member of the Brothers of Herrad, the founder's grandson, Doug

Tamworth. Though that relationship soured after Bradford passed away."

Ben's jaw dropped. "They were thrown out of the Brothers as soon as it became known there were dirty. You think Doug took them in afterward?"

"They were absolutely in contact, multiple times. Billy met with Doug recently, in Kansas. There's no hard evidence of any illegal activity involving Doug, or any member of the Brothers of Herrad."

Ben didn't know what to say. He looked Agent Dario in the eyes, but she could tell he hadn't fully digested her words.

Agent Dario continued, "Do you have any reason to suspect Doug would be involved in something illegal? Would he have any reason to want to harm you?"

Ben regained his focus and shook his head, still in shock at his naiveté. "I can't see Doug being involved in anything with the Sullivans. He has no reason to want to harm me that I can think of. But Billy and his father are masters of manipulation. I mean, they got Ted to turn, for a while anyways. And Ted Seneca is good man."

Ben stopped short of offering any more opinions. He remembered people in Agent Dario's field didn't put much stock in opinion. When Agent Dario asked for a reason to believe, she meant evidence, not opinion. Then a rush of thoughts and emotion overcame him.

Would Doug want me dead? Other than the fact that he wanted to be Worshipful Master, we had no problems, did we? No. And I handed all of that back to his grandfather. Doug has to be the first choice now. He doesn't seem the type to hold a grudge. Why would he come after me now?

Oh, my God, is Mr. James involved in any of this? There's no way he would do anything to hurt me. No way. Billy, on the other hand…

Agent Dario snapped the young man back into focus. "Right now Billy Sullivan has our full attention. We have no reason to go after Doug Tamworth. We're watching every move Billy makes. If he comes within fifty miles of here, I'll be there to intercept him. With plenty of backup, and local authorities. You're perfectly safe. But please, keep me posted if you plan on going too far out of town. I need to know where you are at all times in order to protect you."

Before Agent Dario left him alone, out in the middle of nowhere, with an apparent criminal out to kill him, Ben had one specific question to ask. He didn't think his question would be answered, but the visibly shaken young man felt he needed to try.

"How did I get caught up in all of this? I mean, I know why Billy's out to get me. I get that. But how did these guys find me in the first place? I feel like they came looking for me before I even left Arkansas."

Agent Dario thought about how to answer Ben's question. She could easily satisfy him with an answer that didn't include most of the story. She knew that's how she should answer the question. She knew Ben had more knowledge than most about how things worked behind the closed doors of Federal office buildings. But he didn't know all of it. This could allow her to give what seemed like a perfectly logical explanation, without sharing any sensitive information.

"This is strictly off the record," Agent Dario declared.

"I think you know by now, I can keep a secret," Ben replied.

"Your perception is incredible. The answer to your question goes much further than just landing the right job at the company and excelling to a point that put you next in line to replace Ted Seneca. Bradford Sullivan had connections. Connections that went beyond my level of understanding. He knew why you were recruited for the job at the company. He knew far more than he had a right to know about you, and he used that information to make sure you ended up exactly where you did. So he could exploit you the same way he exploited Ted."

"But how did they come and find me, way out here?" Ben asked.

"The government pays attention to more than just your grades, or your resume. In your case, nearly perfect SAT scores and perfect grades in college put you on a list of potential candidates for highly specialized positions within the Federal Government. That's not enough however. Those qualities may get you a great position in the private sector, but the Federal Government wants to know more. So they use personality testing, private files from your school records, and whatever else they need to get a better idea of how your mind works, how you would handle a specific task, or respond to receiving specific information."

"I've never taken a personality test of any kind. How would they know my personality?"

"You've taken several personality tests, starting in elementary school. You've just come to know them as federal standardized testing."

"That sounds like some conspiracy theory my father would read off the internet and run with. It seems too crazy to be true."

"The Federal Government relies on exactly what you just said for deniability," Agent Dario admitted.

"OK fine. So they used my transcripts and SAT scores as an initial tool, and then they dug deeper and figured out I fit some profile. Why did Bradford Sullivan, or whoever, want me so badly? What's so special about me? Anyone could have taken over for Ted. And they needed a criminal. Do I have some dark personality traits that I don't even know about?"

"No, you don't. If you did, they would never have recruited you. And Bradford knew that. Your personality traits checked all the right boxes for both the Federal Government and Bradford, without any negatives. Your intelligence, work ethic, empathy, loyalty, morality and a few other traits made you an outstanding Intelligence Analyst. The fact that you grew up in poverty and had a strong desire to help other poor people, particularly children, were excellent traits to be manipulated by the Brothers of Herrad. Bradford thought you could be persuaded to look the other way if it meant funding an organization that did so much for the people you cared most about. Bradford would continue to keep federal law enforcement in the dark from the inside, and after Ted retired, you would take over his role and keep the company from blowing the whistle from the outside. That was his plan, but he underestimated you."

It all made perfect sense now. And now more than ever Ben felt pride for walking away from all of it. Even if it meant his friendship with Mr. James would come to an end.

"So the government follows everyone around, gathers all this *personality data,* and picks out the ones they want?" Ben asked.

"Not everyone. Most people don't make the first cut with their public records. Their private information is completely ignored, and they live their lives without ever knowing anything about any of this," Agent Dario answered.

Ben just nodded.

"We're not evil, Ben. The intent is to ensure proper people are chosen for very important positions. Positions that keep us all safe. The system only breaks down when someone like Bradford Sullivan uses it for personal advantage. It's infrequent, but it happens," Agent Dario admitted.

Ben thought about everything Agent Dario had told him. *I'm really glad I asked the question. Now I know I made all the right choices.*

I'm going after what I want now, not what someone else thinks I'd be good at. This is my true calling.

"I have to leave you now, Ben. I have a meeting with local police. I'm working closely with them, and I need to constantly update them on what's happening."

"One last thing before you go. I'm sure you don't know much about it, but how the heck did Angelina Rindge come to be involved with all of this?"

Agent Dario thought about a simple answer, again. Ben would never suspect she knew anything in detail about Angelina Rindge. He certainly didn't know Angelina was in Decatur, keeping out of sight and waiting at the one room apartment Agent Dario temporarily called home, courtesy of the FBI. *She better be keeping out of sight.*

Reina Dario decided to do something completely out of character. Why not? This entire conversation was completely out of character. She decided to get personal.

"Angelina Rindge and Billy Sullivan were close during high school and college. She has no connection with the government beyond that. She just got mixed up with the wrong person and happened to be in DC at the wrong time. The Sullivans manipulated and used her like they did everyone else."

Ben gave a short, but telling laugh. He couldn't hide his feelings for Angelina from anyone. Especially not a trained FBI Agent.

"She's a good kid, Ben. And I happen to know for certain she deeply regrets what happened between the two of you. She's finishing law school in Massachusetts and wants to go into law enforcement when she's done. She's learned from her mistakes, and I think she'll make an excellent colleague in my field. What she did to you may seem inexcusable. Maybe it is. I just hope what I'm telling you makes you feel a little better."

Chapter 37

Mr. James didn't sleep well when something troubled him. The ninety-nine-year-old man knew his stress level had to be managed, so he got out of bed early. Since he still possessed enough strength to handle small amounts exercise he decided to take a short, early-morning walk through the Village of Loch Lloyd community around his grandson's home in Loch Lloyd, Missouri. The Village of Loch Lloyd is a private gated resort-like community, south of Kansas City on the Missouri-Kansas border.

The December air chilled the old man, and the ground was covered sparsely with a light snowfall from the night before. The handful of luxury homes he passed along his short walk, while slowly scuffling his sneakers on the ground, were beautiful, with perfectly manicured lawns and gardens. Most of them were still dark due to the early hour.

The founder of the Brothers of Herrad had reached a tremendously difficult decision recently, but the more time he spent thinking about it, the more comfortable he became with his choice. By the time he made his way back to his grandson's home, his doubts were gone. When Doug Tamworth awoke, his grandfather intended to share some exciting news with him.

"Grandad, what are you doing up so early?" Doug asked, surprised to see his grandfather sitting alone, drinking cold water from a coffee cup.

"At my age, every minute counts. Why waste what precious few I have left staring at a ceiling over a bed I can't sleep in?"

"Are you uncomfortable in the spare bedroom? Is it the lighting in there? It does face the sun. We can do something to block that window better," Doug offered.

"No, Douglas, it's perfectly fine."

"Well, what's going on then? Are you feeling OK?"

"I'm fine. Everything is fine. Are you the only one up? I'd like to have a private conversation with you."

"Um, yeah. Molly's still in bed. The girls don't come until tomorrow. Both Katy and Valarie are coming. You're gonna get to see your great-great granddaughter Brooklyn for the first time. Val called us last night. Her husband Steve was able to pull some strings at work. He's coming with her, too. We'll have a nice visit with the whole family. You are still planning to stay through Christmas right?"

"Yes, of course. I wish your mother could have made it from Boston, but she's spending Christmas with your sisters, as always," Mr. James added.

"It would have been nice to see Mom. I'm sure you would've liked to see your only daughter for the holiday, too, but she and my sisters will have a very nice time with the rest of the family back east."

Mr. James nodded in agreement.

"Grandad, I'm so happy you're with us out here. It's nice that you won't be alone in DC for once."

"That's part of what I'd like to talk to you about. I've made a few decisions that will impact both of our futures."

Doug finished making his cup of coffee and laughed at his grandfather's choice of drinking glass. "Would you like me to get you a glass, with ice?"

"No, no don't bother. This suits me perfectly fine. Have a seat Douglas. Let's talk a minute."

Doug sat down and sipped his coffee. "What's on your mind, Grandad?"

"I'm retiring from the Brothers of Herrad. Not just from my leadership role. I'm no longer going to be active in any capacity. That means I'll no longer be attending assemblies either."

Doug's eyes opened wider, and he stared at his grandfather with excitement. *Does this mean…*

"This means I've also made my decision about who will be the next Worshipful Master. It's you Douglas. You've earned it. The book and the ring are in the top drawer of the bureau, next to the bed in the spare bedroom. They belong to you now. I'd offer my guidance to you on running the organization, but we both know you don't need it." *And I know you won't take it.*

"Grandad, this is wonderful news. I've hoped for this moment since the very first day you described the Brothers of Herrad to me, when I was still in prep school. This means everything to me. I'm so honored," Doug declared.

Mr. James patted his grandson's shoulder but didn't speak any more about the topic. Doug was never his first choice for the position. The younger man cared more about the prestige of the group than he did about its purpose, and that fact troubled the old man from the moment Ben relinquished the title.

The founder once admired his grandson's excellent fundraising abilities. And associations with people like Bradford Sullivan helped to grow the Brothers of Herrad far beyond anything he had ever imagined. Still, Mr. James felt troubled over what the group would become.

The excitement the old man had felt a month ago, when he heard about Ben's bake sale and town dance and the community's response, had faded completely. Under Doug's leadership, the Brothers would return to the type of private organization that raised funds behind closed-door meetings with powerful people and questionable practices.

Mr. James felt he no longer had the time required to change the course of the organization, which took on the same character and focus that caused the old man to leave the Freemason's fifty years earlier. His young friend Ben was his only hope for change and that hope vanished when Ben resigned.

"One more thing, Douglas."

Doug smiled at his beloved grandfather. "Anything, Grandad."

"I'd like your help selling my house in Washington, DC. I'm going home, to Boston. I'd like to be close to your mother and sisters. I'd like to spend my final years there. Can you help me with those arrangements, as quickly as possible?"

Chapter 38

Angelina Rindge lay on top of the blankets, watching Keeping Up with the Kardashians, on the single king-size bed in the room she now shared with Special Agent Dario. The FBI had rented the room at Roller Avenue Apartments in Decatur for Agent Dario so she could be close to Ben. Roller Avenue Apartments looked like a converted roadside motel, with a strip of single-room units. The accommodations were far below any standard Angelina was accustomed to, and the young woman from Boston was getting restless, staring at the four walls, keeping out of sight. She wanted to go see Ben, badly. Even if he didn't want to see her.

"Do you have to lay like that? With your feet on the pillows? You're on my side of the bed, Princess. Scoot!" Agent Dario insisted after returning from her briefing with local law enforcement.

"I'm above the covers, and my feet are clean. I haven't left this room in three days."

"Your clean feet walk on this disgusting floor and look at the comforter. Your giant toes are pulling it down. My pillow isn't covered right now," Agent Dario added.

"Are we having our first fight? Does this mean the honeymoon's over?" Angelina joked, trying to ease the tension.

Agent Dario laughed. Most of the time she enjoyed Angelina's company. Her charm and quick wit made her pleasant to be around. Other times the young woman from Boston reminded the special agent of a spoiled brat who needed a time out, or maybe even a slap on the ass.

Agent Dario's cellphone lit up and vibrated on the nightstand. She didn't receive personal calls, so this had to be either her home office or the local police. Her tone changed immediately to serious and she gave Angelina a look that demanded she remain silent.

Angelina complied.

"Special Agent Dario, the target is on the move. He just made a phone call to arrange purchase of a pistol and silencer. The transaction is scheduled to occur in two and a half hours. We'll text you the address. We have him on record, telling the seller upon receipt of the weapon he'll head south, to eliminate a rat. This is it," the anonymous voice declared.

Agent Dario looked at Angelina and nodded, indicating to her the move on Ben was about to happen.

"Proceed to the meeting place. You're only sixty-five miles south of the location, in Joplin, Missouri. The target is still one hundred fifty miles north. Beat him there and wait. Once he secures the weapon, and begins to move south, you can call the locals and arrest him. No need to allow him to get close to his objective. We have everything we need to make a safe, easy arrest. Are we clear, Agent Dario?"

"Affirmative. We're clear," Agent Dario answered and ended the call.

"OK, Angel. This is it. Billy's making his move. You stay here in this room until I get back, and don't worry. Our plan is to arrest Billy before he even reaches Arkansas. The dumbass gave us a clear confession on his cellphone. We have enough to put him away already. And as usual, he's traveling with his phone. We can track his every move."

Angelina tried to ask more questions, but Agent Dario put her hand up and left. She'd said more than she intended to already. She pointed to Angelina and then to the ground, indicating the civilian needed to stay put.

Chapter 39

Agent Dario sped north on Interstate 49, en route to Joplin, Missouri. The words 'safe, easy arrest' echoed in her mind. She wished the agent on the phone hadn't said that. FBI agents had to be prepared for the worst at all times. Safe and easy were words never spoken while preparing to complete a mission.

A text with the exact location of the weapon transaction came in on the Agent Dario's cellphone. She shook her head when she read the location of the weapon pick up. *Crabby's Seafood Bar and Grill? Oh, Billy, you're such an idiot.*

The young special agent arrived at Crabby's Seafood at 8:30 PM, well ahead of her target. She noticed the restaurant was upscale, nothing like she pictured when she read the name on her cellphone, and there were several expensive cars in the spacious parking lot. There were men, dressed in business casual attire, sitting around the bar. She was unaware of the fact that Billy stopped at Crabby's every time he ventured south, to spy on Ben. *This location makes a little more sense to me now. Blend in, make a quick and quiet transfer and get back on Interstate 49 South. Straight to Ben.*

Don't underestimate this guy. Nothing is ever safe and easy in this profession.

A phone call confirmed Billy would arrive in less than an hour. He was driving his dark-blue Mercedes S-Class Sedan, with his cellphone on hand. *This guy has connections. Hasn't anyone ever told him to leave his phone at home? Safe and easy. This feels too safe and too easy to be true.*

"Right on time, scumbag," Agent Dario said to herself when she noticed Billy's car pull into the parking lot at 9:20 and head to a spot behind the restaurant.

It was too dark to get a positive ID of the driver, but she could tell it was a white male, dressed in a suit, with hair slicked back, corporate executive style. Agent Dario had little doubt about the identity of the driver. If a witness gave her that description alone, she'd know it was Billy. The driver turned off the ignition and waited, alone. He didn't exit the vehicle, and no one else approached it.

Agent Dario stayed focused on the Mercedes while she sat and waited, close by. *I'm in no rush. I have all night.*

Chapter 40

Angelina Rindge couldn't stand being alone in the apartment room any longer. She wanted to go see Ben. She wanted to protect him and tell him everything would be all right. Agent Dario told her the arrest would take place out of state, which meant she'd be gone at least a few hours, and probably several hours longer than that. No one would know she'd gone to Ben. The only thing Angelina had to be concerned about would be Ben slamming a door in her face when she went to see him unannounced.

The young woman from Boston had heard agent Dario repeat Ben's address multiple times while talking to local police on her cellphone. She had it memorized. A quick response from Uber would get her to Ben's apartment in less than ten minutes.

When she got out of the car at the old church building, Angelina looked around and noticed she was in the middle of nowhere. It was dark, quiet, and creepy. She noticed Ben's Jeep Wrangler parked in the driveway. *This is definitely the place. He lives in a church? Well, here goes nothing.*

Ben came to the door after the second ring of the doorbell. He'd been working on the final touches of his journal submission.

He expected to see Reina Dario standing outside when he opened the door.

"Angel? What the heck are you doing here?"

"Surprise?" Angelina said sheepishly.

"Ya think? Yeah, I'm definitely surprised. Why are you here? How did you even get here?" Ben asked looking around and noticing his own car remained the only one in the driveway.

"I'm sorry, Ben, this was a terrible idea. I'm not sure what I'm even doing here," Angelina admitted. She looked like she might start to cry.

"Hey, no, I'm sorry. It's fine. Why don't you come in?"

Angelina followed Ben through the art room and into his apartment. There were papers and books about the Revolutionary War and Dr. Joseph Warren spread out all over his small dining table. Ben laughed nervously and apologized for the mess while clearing the table for them to sit and talk about whatever the heck was on his ex-girlfriend's mind and why she came to Decatur.

"Is this the same little table you had back in Virginia?" Angelina asked with a laugh.

"No, believe it or not. The only thing I took home from Virginia were clothes and bad memories," Ben answered, feeling immediate regret for the last part of his comment. "But it sure does look like it, doesn't it? You want something to drink? I'm afraid all I have is beer, water, and diet soda," Ben offered, quickly changing the subject.

"I'll have a beer." Angelina felt the sting of Ben's words, but also felt encouraged about being inside his apartment. She hadn't expected to get this far.

Ben returned to the table with two beers and glasses, but Angelina pushed her glass aside and took a surprisingly long drink directly from the bottle.

"Thirsty?" Ben laughed. "I guess if I walked here from Boston, I'd want a beer, too."

Angelina decided a little small talk would be best before she informed Ben that Billy was about to get arrested a hundred miles north, for plotting to kill him with a silent pistol.

"So, Ben, how've you been? You seeing anybody?" Angelina asked.

"I was seeing Patty after we broke up. She even came out here for a visit, but that didn't work out," Ben answered and then tried to redirect the conversation. "Angel? What the hell are you doing here?"

Angelina attempted to ignore the question a little longer. "Patty? Yeah, I can understand that. She's beautiful. I thought about taking a run at her myself," Angelina laughed. "Awkward! Huh, Babe?"

Ben tried to give Angelina a cold stare, but a smile jumped onto his face. He couldn't help it. *Babe?*

"Are you gonna tell me why you're here? *Babe*?" Ben persisted.

Just as Angelina began the long explanation of her visit, the two heard a beeping sound coming from underneath the couch just a few feet away, and then something that sounded like air deflating from a car tire, at fast rate.

Ben got up to go and look under the couch but stumbled to the floor. Before he passed out, he looked up and noticed Angelina slumped over the small table.

Chapter 41

Agent Dario started to feel uneasy. She waited for three hours, and nothing happened. There was no movement from inside Billy's vehicle, and no one came anywhere near the car from the outside. The restaurant closed at 10:00, and everyone went home by 11:00, including staff. Besides her rental, Billy's was the only car in the parking lot. *I'm completely out in the open here. He's probably already noticed me. He hasn't moved for almost two hours. No phone calls, nothing. What the hell is he waiting for? Did his contact stand him up? He was supposed to be here at 9:30. It's almost midnight.*

The special agent decided she needed to make a move. She'd drive by the car, slowly, and glance over to see if she could tell what Billy was doing, and then find a spot off the road, toward the highway to wait for him to pass by on his way to Decatur. Once he got on the highway, she'd make the move to arrest him.

"Oh, shit!" Agent Dario shouted to herself when she got close enough to the Mercedes to see the driver slumped over the steering wheel, and the windows fogged up from the inside of the vehicle.

The special agent stopped her car and ran over to Billy's. She knocked loudly on the driver's side window, but Billy didn't move. She tried to open the door, but it was locked. Agent Dario pulled out her pistol, shot out the rear window and reached in to unlock the doors.

Billy didn't move after the shot was fired. Agent Dario checked his neck for a pulse, but there wasn't one. And then she noticed something. *Holy shit. This isn't Billy Sullivan! That motherfucker!*

While looking over the body for signs of injury, Agent Dario noticed a strange looking air freshener attached to the air vent closest to the driver. It looked broken and hollow, as if its contents had been emptied out. Then she immediately got out of the car and pulled out her cellphone. She'd seen a device like that before.

"This is Special Agent Reina Dario. We've been duped. The target is not at my location. The man here is dead. I repeat, the target is off the grid. Suspected hydrogen cyanide poisoning of decoy, released remotely from a device planted in the vehicle. We've seen this type of device before. This is sophisticated stuff. Whoever gave Billy this device isn't fucking around. Billy's not smart enough to pull this off on his own. Call locals to my location immediately, with hazmat crew. And get the authorities in Decatur on the phone right away. Ben Gilsum is alone in the dark! My ETA to his location is one hour."

Chapter 42

Ben awoke in a fog, on his bed, with a strong smell of alcohol in the air. His head hurt, and his vision was severely blurred. He tried to rub his eyes, but couldn't move. As he started to become more aware of his surroundings, he realized he and Angelina were tied together, bound back to back by their ankles and below their shoulders. Their arms were tied tightly to their sides. The two were stripped down to their underwear. *What the hell is going on here?*

Finally able to lift his head a little and look around, Ben noticed Billy Sullivan standing at the foot of the bed, smiling at him.

"Well, good morning, sunshine," Billy said with a grin. "And look at this, your girlfriend's here, too. I certainly wasn't expecting to see Angel today. Two rats for the price of one? What a deal."

"Billy, what are you doing? Is Angel OK?" Ben asked, still in a cloud.

"Hmm, now that's a great question Ben. What *am* I doing?" Billy asked. "I'm settling an old score, asshole. That's what I'm doing. And Angel is fine, for now. She'll wake up any minute. I had to pump enough halothane into the air to take down a big boy like you. I didn't plan for a beauty queen."

"What are you gonna do with us?" Ben asked as Billy began pouring a clear liquid all over the room.

"You'll probably start to feel a little hot in a minute. And not just because you're tied to a beautiful naked woman. Wait, smell that? Is that smoke? I think there's a fire upstairs. You know the wiring in old buildings causes all sorts of terrible tragedies."

Billy took a drink from the bottle he'd been pouring and poured more of the liquid onto the bed. He splashed it all over Ben and Angelina.

"Two young lovers, getting drunk on Everclear. It's pretty strong stuff. Did you know you can only get 190 proof in twenty-five states? And Arkansas happens to be one of them. It's highly flammable," Billy added, taking another drink then tossing the empty bottle to the floor.

The alcohol burned Ben's eyes. He shut them tight and shook his head, unable to get his hands to his face to rub them.

"The young couple probably passed out on the bed while the building burned down around them. I soaked your bindings in it too, so they'll be gone before anyone finds what's left of you. This stuff burns like gasoline but leaves no reason to suspect foul play. There's a couple bottles in the fridge, too. The garbage can outside's full of beer and wine bottles. Just to drive the point home."

Ben didn't speak, he tried in vain to untie himself and get to Billy.

"You know what the best part of all of this is? Your friend from the FBI thought I was a total idiot. Yet she fell for the old bait and switch. Your guardian angel is sixty miles away, waiting for a dead man to come and get you. You know he's driving a stolen car? At least I reported it stolen after I paid him to dress up like me, and drive to my favorite restaurant. I told him I'd show up at exactly 9:30 with further instruction, so he'd better be there on time if he wanted more cash. Wait a minute, come to think of it, I've never seen him before in my life, but I like his hair. And he's a pretty snappy dresser, too. You know the bastard even took my cellphone?" Billy laughed. "I had to drive all the way here off the grid in an old pickup truck that I borrowed off some redneck that I'll return on my way home. And he won't remember who I am. I think he got drunk and passed out, too. Alcohol poisoning? You know I coulda waved at Special Agent Dario on the highway on the way here, but why add insult to injury?"

Ben began to feel Angelina moving as she started to wake up. He yelled out to Billy, "Why don't you let her go? She didn't do anything to you."

"That's not true!" Billy shouted. "She's a rat, just like you. She's the one who went to the FBI. She still loves you, Benny. She's also, unfortunately, at the wrong place at the *very* wrong time."

Billy noticed Angelina was looking at him, squinting, "Hi, Honey. Welcome to the conversation. You picked a really shitty night to go and see your boyfriend, didn't you?"

Angel struggled to pull her hands out of her bindings, but couldn't. "What the fuck, Billy?"

"Anyway, you two aren't the only ones with resourceful friends. I got some really cool toys and great ideas from mine and it's been a true pleasure using them," Billy added as he pulled a lighter and handkerchief out of his pocket.

"Billy, don't do this!" Angelina yelled, crying.

"I'd love to prolong this and listen to the two of you beg me to stop, but I think it's only a matter of time before someone at the FBI catches on and we have company. Besides, this building is about to fall apart. By the way, love what you've done with the place, Benny."

Billy struggled to light the lighter while wearing gloves and removed one to light the handkerchief, but before it caught fire a loud bang sounded behind him. He dropped the unlit lighter and handkerchief harmlessly onto the floor, and his body arched forward in agony.

Billy spun around to look behind him as he fell, "Doug? But I thought you decided to help me?"

Doug Tamworth rushed into the room. The fire upstairs raged and the ceiling above the first floor appeared ready give way at any moment. He untied Ben and Angelina, helping them to their feet.

"We need to get out of here, right now!" Doug shouted.

"I need my clothes," Angelina cried, looking around the floor.

Doug grabbed the alcohol soaked blanket and sheet off the bed, and threw them to Ben and Angelina. "These will have to do. Let's go!"

The trio stepped around Billy, making their way outside.

"Should we get him out of here?" Angelina asked, pointing to Billy.

"I'm sure he's dead!" Doug shouted. "There's no time!"

Once outside they could hear sirens approaching from far away, slowly getting closer. Moments later local police and the fire department arrived as the first-floor ceiling collapsed. The entire building became engulfed in flames.

Ben watched in agony as the fire department doused the flames consuming the old church building. By the time they extinguished the fire, there was very little left standing. The Decatur Club for Boys and Girls, a project Ben had put his heart and soul behind and planned to open in two weeks was reduced to a pile of smoldering ash. His heart was broken, again.

Angelina put her hand on Ben's shoulder. "I'm so sorry, Ben. This is awful."

Ben felt comfort in Angelina's words and then noticed she no longer had the whiskey-soaked blanket Doug tossed her as they escaped the fire. The young woman was dressed in active wear that appeared to be two sizes too small.

"Where on Earth did you get those clothes?" Ben asked.

"You like? A female officer let me borrow them. She's a little shorter than I am," Angelina smiled, spinning around in workout clothes the officer had in her trunk.

Ben smiled back. Angelina always had an uncanny way to bring light to the darkest of moments. It seemed impossible for Ben to not feel some measure of joy when he was near her. He'd forgotten all his questions about why Angelina came to Arkansas. None of that mattered anymore.

A car pulled into the driveway and Reina Dario stepped out, running toward Ben and Angelina.

Agent Dario shot an angry look at Angelina but quickly turned her focus to Ben. "Are you OK? I'm so sorry I failed you. I can't believe I allowed this to happen."

"I'm fine. Angelina's fine. Somewhere in that mess, you'll find Billy. Doug Tamworth put a bullet in him before he could finish us off."

"What? What the hell is Doug Tamworth doing here?" Agent Dario asked, confused. "Where is he?"

"He's over there talking to the cops. I'm sure they're asking him the same question. Personally, I'm pretty happy he showed up," Ben replied.

Agent Dario moved quickly to the group of officers that were questioning Doug Tamworth and took control of the inquiry.

"I'm taking Mr. Tamworth into FBI custody. Doug come with me, right now," Agent Dario demanded and led him to the passenger seat of her car. She closed the door and walked away from everyone to make a phone call.

Ben watched Agent Dario argue with whoever she was speaking with on her cellphone, but he couldn't hear anything. She appeared frustrated, occasionally looking up at the black sky and shaking a fist with her free hand. She ended her call, shook her head, and then walked over to the group of officers. Ben and Angelina moved closer so they could hear what Agent Dario said.

"I've been instructed to take Mr. Tamworth to the FBI office in Kansas City. They're taking over all further communication with him. I'm sorry, but he can no longer give you a statement. Whatever he said before is off the record. I need your notes, now. Any questions you have should be directed to the FBI. I'm not to question him either."

A puzzled officer asked, "You're just gonna leave then? We have a lot of questions. What about these two," he asked, pointing to Ben and Angelina.

"You're free to question Mr. Gilsum and Miss Rindge after I have a private moment with them. Wrap it up, though. They need to get to a hospital to be checked out. I'm not to leave here until I confirm Billy Sullivan is dead," Agent Dario added.

The local police officers moved away, giving the special agent her requested privacy with Ben and Angelina.

"Angel, I'm not even going to ask you why you're here. I'll take full responsibility for putting you in harm's way. That's all I'm going to say to you on that topic."

Agent Dario shifted her gaze to Ben. "The FBI's probably not going to question Doug Tamworth. He'll walk away, but we both know he's involved somehow in what happened here tonight. This stinks like DC all over again. I felt you deserved to know. We're gonna have to let this one go, Ben. Just be thankful you're alive."

"Are you kidding me? I think he planned all of it. Billy mentioned he had resourceful friends with great toys. After Doug shot him, Billy even mentioned he was helping him. This sucks, Reina!" Ben shouted, catching the attention of a few police officers.

"I agree, but lower your voice. Let it go Ben. It's over now. It's out of our hands. Don't repeat what you just told me to the police. This ends here. Billy acted alone and now he's dead. You're safe, and that's all that matters. Can I trust you to follow me on this?"

Ben reluctantly agreed.

"One more thing," Agent Dario added. "Can you see to it that Angelina gets back to my apartment quickly, to pick up her belongings, and then on a plane back to Boston as soon as possible?"

"Special Agent Dario, the body's missing. There's no one in the building!" a police officer shouted.

"You've got to be fucking kidding me," Agent Dario responded as Ben and Angelina looked at each other in horror.

Chapter 43

The horror Ben experienced after hearing Billy had somehow survived being shot and the fire was short-lived. Special Agent Dario had put Ben and Angelina in the back of a squad car to keep them safe, and demanded all the local officers spread out and search the property for any signs of Billy Sullivan. His body was quickly discovered only fifty feet from the church building. He had crawled into the woods and succumbed to his injuries in the darkness, alone.

With her assignment in Arkansas wrapped up, Agent Dario returned to her Washington, DC office.

Two days after the fire, Ben tried to rest on the short, uncomfortable couch at his father's house, where he'd be staying until he figured out what to do next. As he had promised Agent Dario, Ben helped Angelina get her belongings from the Roller Avenue Apartments, but Angelina checked into a room in Bentonville before booking a flight home. She insisted Ben spend a day with her, which he did, to discuss everything that had happened to them in regard to the Sullivans. Angelina also insisted that the night before she left town, she have dinner with the Gilsum family. Once Ben reluctantly agreed, she booked a flight back to Boston, which was scheduled to leave the next day.

Ben found it easier than expected to forgive Angelina, considering she had risked her life to save him, but he remained uneasy about forming a more serious relationship. The pain he had experienced in Alexandria was still fresh in his mind.

"She's really comin' over tonight? I'm finally gonna meet your Angel?" an excited Mr. Gilsum asked his son.

"Yes, Dad. The one and only Angel is coming for dinner. She's only in town until tomorrow, and she's coming over here tonight."

"I know she'd stay here with us awhile longer if you weren't a bonehead and broke her heart back in Virginia," Mr. Gilsum declared.

Ben didn't bother correcting his father and just smiled. "Know what, Dad? You're probably right."

"I'll make something special for you, Ben. You name it. I'll pick it up and have it prepared for you and your lovely guest tonight. Lemme see what we got in the kitchen, and then we can make a list together," Aunt Lilian promised and went into the kitchen.

Ben smiled and looked at his father, who immediately looked away. "You two seem to be getting along a lot better these days. No fighting? No arguing? What's going on there, Dad? You finally warming up to the she-devil?"

Mr. Gilsum just gave a short chuckle and shook his head, not making eye contact.

The young man gave Aunt Lilian his dinner request, a southern favorite for his friend from Boston to try; fried catfish with rice and okra. He thanked his Aunt with a hug and then made his way to Bentonville to pick up the family's dinner guest. *I can't wait to see her face when she looks at that catfish. Bet she won't even touch it. This should be hilarious.*

"I have a surprise for you Angel," Ben declared on the drive back to his father's house.

"Oh really? I don't know if we can handle any more surprises, but let's hear it Babe," Angelina replied.

"I'm flying to Boston with you tomorrow."

"You're what? Um, Ben, are you feeling OK?"

"I'm doing very well, thanks for asking. It's probably nothing, but I'd kick myself if I didn't at least take a good look. The head of the history department at Tufts, in Boston, is flying me out to talk about the possibility of teaching there."

"Tufts? The medical school?" Angelina asked.

"Yes, that Tufts. They also have a damn good history department," Ben added. "A professor in my master's program told them all about me and they asked if I'd come for an interview. I'm happy at John Brown University, so this is really just a welcome distraction for a couple days. I don't expect much."

Angelina smiled and looked out the window for the rest of the ride to Decatur.

Chapter 44

Ben watched for Angelina's reaction as they pulled into the driveway of the small, humble home he grew up in. *No way the socialite from Boston is gonna be comfortable out here in the woods of Arkansas. Not sure what I was thinking bringing her here, but at least I'll know if she's sincere when I see how she handles our little diner.*

Angelina looked at Ben with a bright, beautiful smile. "It's so cute. This is exactly the way I pictured it. I can't wait to meet your father."

The beautiful dinner guest from Boston lit up the room in Decatur as she'd done in every room Ben had ever seen her in. Any anxiety he felt about having Angelina at his house vanished as she charmed everyone and kept the conversation active and entertaining.

"Son, I think she's the prettiest girl I've ever laid eyes on. And she's definitely the most pleasant creature I ever met," Mr. Gilsum declared, when Angelina excused herself to offer assistance to Aunt Lilian in the kitchen.

Ben just smiled and nodded.

"You got yourself a second chance here. You don't need me to tell you this, but I'm gonna do it anyway cause I'm your father and I love you. Don't blow it. Life don't offer many an opportunity for a second chance. Take it, Son."

The young man's eyes welled up, but it had nothing to do with Mr. Gilsum's mention of a second chance with Angelina. At twenty-four years old, Ben couldn't remember the last time his father told him he loved him. It's possible he never did, but Ben always knew it and didn't think he needed to hear the words. Until he heard them. *What's going on with the old man? He just came out and said it, freely, like he'd been saying it for years.*

Ben felt a powerful rush of emotion come over him and could barely contain himself. He smiled at his father, fighting back the tears.

"Dinner is served, gentlemen," Angelina announced, returning to the table with Aunt Lilian.

"What do you think, Angel?" Ben asked, referring to the fried catfish and sliced okra.

"What do I think? I think I'm starving, and I've never seen such an amazing home-cooked meal in my entire life. Aunt Lilian, it looks incredible. Thanks so much for having me."

Before the foursome finished their meal, there was a faint tapping at the front door. Ben heard the familiar sound first and got up to go and answer the door.

"Tell them to go away. I'm having too much fun with Miss Angel to be bothered by unwanted company," Mr. Gilsum shouted as Ben reached the front door.

Ben knew who it was before he got there but didn't believe it until he opened the door and saw his old friend Mr. James standing there in his familiar wool pants and sweater.

"Mr. James, how did you get here?" Ben asked, seeing an empty car with Kansas City plates parked in the driveway.

"I drove from my grandson's house in Kansas City. I borrowed his wife's car, without asking. She'll be fine."

Ben looked at his old friend, stunned. *The old man drove alone? All the way from Kansas City?*

"I needed to see you before I left the area. I heard about the club. What can I do to help? Anything Ben, just name it, Son," Mr. James offered.

Ben stepped outside and shut the door behind him. "The club is completely destroyed and I'm not planning to rebuild it. Once the authorities complete their investigation, I intend to donate the land to Decatur Parks and Recreation along with the funds you gave the club and the insurance money from the fire. I'd like them to build a playground and maybe even a small waterpark there and use the fields for youth sports. The kids around here would love that. This will terminate my involvement with the Brothers of Herrad, completely. That's what I want. Unless of course you'd like the money back," Ben added.

Mr. James tried, but failed to hide the pain Ben's words brought him. "The money is yours to do with what you wish. I don't want it back."

"I just don't know who to trust anymore. I'm sorry, Mr. James. I don't know how far all of this went or who knew what. I sincerely don't believe you had anything to do with any of the bad stuff. And if you did, I'd rather not know about it. Thank you for everything, but I need to get away from all of this and start living life on my own terms."

Ben tried to continue, but his voice began to crack and he couldn't get the words out. "I can't. I'm sorry," Ben said and turned to go back into the house to rejoin Angelina and his family.

Angelina stood in Ben's way as he tried to go back inside the house. She peeked around Ben to see Mr. James standing there with tears in his eyes.

"He's not with them, Ben," she said. "He's never been with any of them. They used him, the same way they used you, and the same way they used me. Look at him. You know it's true. He's a good man."

Ben turned and looked at Mr. James, who tried to force a smile. Somehow the young man knew Angelina's words were true. He went back and gave his friend a long hug, and then a handshake.

"Mr. James do you need someone to drive you back to Kansas City?" Ben asked.

"No, don't you worry about me. I'll be fine. You're one in a million, Son. Good luck with your teaching. You'll make an outstanding college professor. I'd like to leave you with one last piece of advice if I may."

"Of course, Mr. James."

"You should stop worrying about whether you deserve the many blessings in your life, and start enjoying them to the fullest. Goodbye, Ben."

"Goodbye, Mr. James," Ben replied with tears in his eyes.

Before he made his way to his daughter-in-law's car, to make the long drive back to Kansas City alone, Angelina ran over and gave Mr. James an affectionate hug. She knew exactly what a firm goodbye from Ben felt like. And though she helped to soften the blow for Mr. James with her actions and words, she still felt the need to comfort the old man.

Mr. James whispered faintly into her ear, "Thank you, Angelina. And don't you give up on him. He still loves you. It's as obvious to me as the look on his face. I wish you both many years of happiness."

The young woman from Boston gave Mr. James a soft kiss on the cheek.

Chapter 45

The middle seat, on the late-night flight from Northwest Arkansas Regional to Logan Airport in Boston, couldn't provide Ben with enough comfort to sleep. The young man hadn't slept well since his encounter with Billy Sullivan, and his father's couch gave him aches and pains to go along with the nerves he still felt after the attack. He felt fortunate to have a seat at all, with the last-minute flight purchase from Tufts University, just a few days before Christmas.

Ben looked back a few rows and saw Angelina fast asleep in a window seat. The beautiful young woman had acquired the favorable seat by trade, with an older gentleman who wouldn't take no for an answer. The gentleman now sat wide awake in the middle seat next to her, smiling and nodding at Ben as he checked on his friend.

Ben smiled back and faced forward. He planned on re-finishing his history journal submission on the flight. All the work completed the night of the attack was lost in the fire, along with his laptop, but thankfully he'd emailed himself a draft the day before. The habit of saving and emailing himself a copy with every writing session, saved the young man an incredible amount of effort.

A new laptop and an excellent memory made it easy to pick up where he left off. The cramped quarters he found himself trapped in, however, did not allow Ben the comfort needed to work on the plane as he planned. So he sat there, with a fellow passenger on either side of him, each fully occupying the armrest between them, with his arms crossed and his eyes closed, for the rest of the flight.

The plane touched down at Logan Airport just after midnight, twenty minutes ahead of schedule. Ben got off first and waited in the gate area for Angelina to come out.

"There you are. I thought you left me in the dust," Angelina declared.

"No. I wouldn't do that to you twice," Ben joked.

"Ouch, Babe. Funny yes, but ouch."

"Well, *Babe.* I have a car picking me up at Ground Transportation, courtesy of Tufts University. I should head that way so the driver can get to bed before the sun comes up."

"You have my number, Professor. And we're good right?"

"I do. And yes, we're good."

"Good. Call me before you leave town. And not from the airport. I want you for an afternoon, or even an early evening, before you go back to Arkansas. Promise me."

"I promise," Ben replied.

Ben turned and started to walk away but stopped. He turned back and saw Angelina standing exactly where he left her, smiling at him.

"You know, I never found out why you came to Arkansas."

Angelina started to answer, but Ben interrupted her.

"Don't tell me. I don't need to know anymore. Thank you for coming for me and trying to protect me. And especially, thank you for not giving up," Ben added.

"I'll never give up," Angelina answered with tears in her dark blue eyes. "You can count on that. And when you're ready, I'll be here for you. Don't take too long, OK, Babe?"

Ben smiled and wrapped Angelina in a long embrace.

"You got it, *Babe." Or should I call you my Angel. My Guardian Angel.*

A twenty minute limo ride to Hyatt Place in Medford, a hotel just a mile away from Tufts University, carried the exhausted young man from Arkansas to a comfortable bed, where he enjoyed his first restful sleep in four nights.

Chapter 46

Ben arrived at Tufts University early to walk around and get a good feel for the campus. The December snow cover, gray sky, and bare trees didn't offer much color, but Ben was impressed with how he didn't feel like he was only five miles away from Downtown Boston. *I expected to be in the middle of the city, but this isn't that bad. It's a lot colder than Siloam Springs, but this campus is nice. I could see myself working here. And taking classes here.*

The young man sipped the last of the coffee he took in a to-go cup from the breakfast buffet at Hyatt Place and studied his campus map. *East Hall? Where the heck is East Hall?*

Ben arrived at East Hall fifteen minutes early, but that didn't bother Doctor Marcus Alstead, who greeted the young man with a smile and enthusiastic handshake.

Marcus Alstead, head of the history department at Tufts University, was a short, thin man with peppered-gray hair behind a receding hairline which exaggerated the size of his forehead. He wore brown, large-framed glasses and a bow tie that appeared extra-large on the very thin man's neck.

"Mr. Gilsum, it's a pleasure to meet you. Doctor Hinsdale has told me so much about you. You've made quite an impression on him. How was your flight?" Dr. Alstead spoke in a high-pitched, nasal voice as he led Ben to a small conference room.

"It was perfect, Dr. Alstead. We arrived ahead of schedule," Ben answered, not bothering to complain about his uncomfortable seating arrangements.

"Please call me Marcus if you wouldn't mind. We have enough medical doctors and dentists here at Tufts. Let them have that title. I like being called by my first name, it makes me feel different," Dr. Alstead added with a laugh that concluded with a subtle snort.

"That works for me, Marcus. And you can call me Ben instead of Mr. Gilsum if you prefer."

"Let's see how much I like you first, Mr. Gilsum," Marcus answered with another laugh and snort.

Ben expected to be asked all the same types of questions he had received at John Brown University from Dr. Orchard during his interview there. He had a lecture prepared and even a grading system and syllabus with him to offer during his interview with Marcus. None of which seemed necessary during the very informal conversation.

"Mr. Gilsum, I already know you're qualified to teach here. We've done an extensive background check, and the president of the university and I had two conference calls with Dr. Franklin Hinsdale, weeks ago, to discuss your credentials. You know he used to teach here, before he went on to become so well known. He and our president are still very close. You don't have the typical resume we've come to expect with new teaching hires, but a glowing recommendation from Franklin Hinsdale goes a long way. Dr. Hinsdale was my teacher and mentor. There isn't a more respected professional in our field."

Ben didn't respond. He didn't know what to say, so he nodded and smiled, awkwardly.

"I'd just like to chat with you for a while if you don't mind. Then you'll meet with a few of our other professors and staff. Relax, be yourself. We just wanna see how you might fit in," Marcus declared with yet another laugh and snort.

Ben felt relieved at first, but then thought, *small talk? I'd rather be grilled with tough questions.*

The shy young man from Arkansas did his best to relax and charm Marcus. It didn't take long for Ben to open up when the topic of his paper for the history journal became part the conversation. He described his theories with enthusiasm and Marcus enjoyed hearing about them. Ben explained his moderate frustration with Dr. Orchard and how he felt restrained due to his current boss's fears of rejection from the academic community.

"Let me assure you, Mr. Gilsum, we won't hold you back at Tufts. I like your ideas. They're original and believable. We'll never know if your theories are true, but as long as they hold water, and are presented as opinions based on fact, they're welcome here. American history is exciting and filled with incredible characters. We want people here who mine all that wonderful information for gold. And I think you're doing just that."

Ben liked the department head's enthusiasm. Marcus seemed like a boss that would be easy to work for, and Ben had a hundred more theories to share, if someone wanted to hear them.

After a few pleasant conversations with two professors and an administrative assistant, Ben waited alone in the small conference room for Marcus to return and conclude the interview process. *This was the strangest interview I've ever had. I kinda liked it.*

"Ben, you did a great job here today. I just had a quick follow-up with my colleagues and it's unanimous," Marcus announced as he entered the room.

He just called me Ben. I guess he likes me.

"You're probably flying back to Arkansas today or tomorrow. I can't get you here for a follow up, so I'm gonna get right to it. We all think you'd be a great fit. I'm making you an offer to start here next semester. You'd assist only, for a semester, and begin teaching classes on your own in the fall of next year if all goes well. How would you like to be an Assistant Professor at Tufts University?" Dr. Alstead asked, and paused to see Ben's reaction. "It gets better, Ben. We're also willing to pay for your education here in Boston, to complete your master's program. Not bad right?" Marcus asked with a big smile, but thankfully no laugh and snort.

Ben stared at Marcus, stunned, unable to speak. He hadn't anticipated any offer at all, certainly not one so quickly. He couldn't find the words to respond. *This doesn't make any sense. I've never taught a class, at any level. I was lucky to get the job at JBU, and now this?*

"I know what you're thinking. How can this be happing so quickly, right? Ben, you're a bit of a rare find. And there's been a lot of buzz generated about you, thanks to Franklin Hinsdale. John Brown University was fortunate enough to know you, and smart enough to reel you in. Personally, I believe Tufts would be a much better fit for you. Don't answer me now, take a few days. If you could let me know before Christmas Eve, which is next week, that would be perfect."

Ben left Tufts University in a haze. *I can't believe what just happened. They actually offered me a job? After one meeting?*

As he promised, Ben called Angelina when he got back to his hotel room. His flight back home wasn't until the next morning so the two could spend the rest of the day together before he left Boston.

"So how'd it go? Did they love you?" Angelina asked.

Ben paused, not ready to tell her they offered him a job. That fact hadn't fully sunken in yet, and he had no idea whether he'd accept or not.

"Shit!"

"Shit? That bad, huh?" Angelina replied.

"No, there's a tag hanging from the arm of my sports coat. I just bought this thing yesterday. All my clothes were burned up in the fire."

"Dork!" Angelina shouted playfully with a loud laugh. "That's hilarious, Babe. I'm sure that made an excellent impression on the people at Tufts."

Ben didn't answer. He wrestled with the tag and yanked it off his sports coat. *Apparently it did.*

"You know, that gives me an excellent idea about what we should do for the rest of your time here in Boston," Angelina declared.

"Really? And what's that? And don't tell me…"

"Shopping spree!" Angelina shouted with glee.

Chapter 47

Miranda Swanzey smiled at Ben from across a high-top table at the Creekside Taproom in Siloam Springs on the Saturday before Christmas. She had invited him to come and celebrate the completion of the painting project at the Community Room. Ben hadn't found the time to go and check it out, but was anxious to see the completed project.

"You look good, Ben. The new clothes suit you. Not exactly my style, but I have to admit, you have excellent taste. Much better than the skinny-boy suits you've been wearing around like some kinda GQ model."

"Angel picked out everything I have on," Ben admitted with a smile, dressed in more casual attire which included jeans, an untucked dress shirt and wool sports coat. His customary slim-fit suits were lost in the fire.

"Ah, you spent some time with Angel. That's nice. It also explains the huge smile on your face and atypical pleasant demeanor. And how about your visit with Tufts?"

"They offered me a position as an Assistant Professor."

Miranda nearly spit out her beer mid-sip, but got it down with a hard gulp, "Are you kidding me? Ben, that's terrific. A round of shots on me."

"I haven't decided if I'm taking the job or not. I have until Monday to let them know."

"Oh, my friend, you've decided. If you could see yourself, you'd know it's pretty obvious. You're going to Boston. And you're not just going there for Tufts either," Miranda predicted.

Ben looked at the smile on Miranda's face. She was happy and excited for him, even with the likelihood of him leaving town. She seemed to care more about his happiness than the prospect of losing a friend. He wondered what might happen between them if he stayed in Arkansas. Was he really locked in the friend zone?

"Miranda you're my best friend. Shit, you're my only friend, actually. Tell me honestly, do you really think I should pack up and head out of here again?"

"I'd love it if you stayed, but that wouldn't be the best thing for you. You need to go to Boston. Don't overthink this like you do with *everything.* You don't fit at the very Christian and conservative John Brown University, and neither do I. We both know that's true. And let's face another very important fact. You're still in love with Miss Angelina Rindge."

Ben stared at the table-top, unable to deny what Miranda just told him. "If I do go to Boston, and it's only an if right now, it's not gonna be about Angel. I promise you that. But if I do go, can

I call you once in a while?" Ben asked, realizing he would still benefit from his best friend's advice.

Miranda didn't answer Ben's question directly. She gave him a warm-reassuring smile instead and declared a toast, "To following your true calling."

What am I gonna tell Dr. Orchard? Forget him, what am I gonna tell my dad?

Chapter 48

Ben stopped at the Community Center in Decatur on his way out of town. His Jeep Wrangler was packed to the roof with new clothes and what little else he could fit for the long drive to Boston. Classes for the spring semester began in two short weeks, on January 16th at Tufts University.

The newly named Assistant Professor of History at Tufts University finally found the time to check out the freshly painted Community Room. He stood alone with the events of the past week buzzing around in his mind like bees competing to enter their nest.

The conversation with his father during Christmas dinner buzzed in the forefront.

"Dad, Aunt Lilian. I have an announcement to make."

He feared a non-reaction from his father, a response that Ben was all too familiar with.

Mr. Gilsum looked his son in the eye. "Boy you'd be a dang fool if you passed up the opportunity to be a college professor in Boston."

Privately, away from Aunt Lilian, an emotionally torn Ben spoke with his father about the move. "Dad, I'm not sure I can do this again, especially with Mom being gone. I can't leave you out here alone. Why don't you come with me?" Ben pleaded, remembering his father had just told him he loved him for the first time in his life only a week before.

"I recon I'll stay here in Decatur, with Aunt Lilian. She's been good to me, Son. All that carryin' on we done before was just for sport. She's a good woman. Maybe I'll even let her drag me into church on Sunday. You find as many excuses as you can to get back here and see us. And bring your Angel with you, you hear?"

Ben smiled to himself, knowing his father would be cared for in his absence. He decided to give something a shot and see how it played out. "I will, Dad, I promise. I love you."

A stunned and tearful Mr. Gilsum returned the sentiment. "Love you too."

"We'll be here for Easter. That's a promise, old man," Ben said as he gave his father a much needed and surprisingly welcomed hug.

The difficult conversation with Dr. Orchard came to mind next.

Ben called his boss and asked if they could meet at his office on campus after Christmas. Dr. Orchard thought his prize new hire wanted to hand him a copy of his completed history journal submission, and happily scheduled the meeting.

"Dr. Orchard, I'm so sorry to have to tell you this. I've lost sleep about it and I feel absolutely terrible. I'll be forever grateful to you for believing in me and giving me such an amazing opportunity. I don't even know how to say this."

"What are trying to tell me Mr. Gilsum?" Dr. Orchard asked, with a dumbfounded look on his face.

"I've received an offer to teach at Tufts University, in Boston. It's a great opportunity for me, and one I couldn't turn down."

"Tufts? The medical school?"

"They have an incredible history department too, Franklin Hinsdale used to…"

"I know, Mr. Gilsum, I was just making a joke," Dr. Orchard said and let out a heavy sigh. "I don't really know how to respond to this news. I had you in to teach Early American History in two weeks. This creates a bit of a problem for us here."

Ben became frantic. "I'm so sorry. I wasn't expecting this to happen. It all came together so quickly. I'm still in shock myself. I hate that I'm doing this to you, maybe…"

"Stop. Don't apologize. Don't rethink or regret your decision. Go to Boston, Mr. Gilsum. It's a great opportunity. I'm very proud of you. I'll find someone to teach your class, or teach it myself. We're going to be just fine here."

Ben calmed down and reached out to shake Dr. Orchard's hand. The professor gave him a prolonged stare and wrapped him in a hug instead.

"Don't be a stranger, Mr. Gilsum. I wish you the best, Son. You'll always have family at John Brown."

Ben's thoughts of the past week faded and he refocused his attention to the beautifully painted red, yellow, and black Kansas City Southern locomotive stretched across the Community Room walls along with the image of the restored depot station with purple flowering tree out front. *Is that a Magnolia tree? A Dogwood maybe?*

He could picture Miranda there, in a long cotton skirt with embroidered flowers and sandals, painting the room with her local students who volunteered time during their winter break to help. He could still sense the warm, pleasant smile on Miranda's face that had filled the room.

This is perfect. Absolutely perfect. I'm really gonna miss you, Miranda. Thank you for this.

Chapter 49

Eleven hours into the fifteen hundred mile drive to Boston, somewhere east of Indianapolis on Highway 70, Ben hit the scan button on his radio, trying to find a song he could sing along with to help keep his eyes open and fight the urge to stop for the night ahead of his planned break in Ohio.

The young traveler laughed to himself when the scan stopped on a country station, playing Willie Nelson's *On the Road Again.*

Ben sang along for the first few verses, then turned the radio down and pulled out his cell phone. He dialed Angelina Rindge's number and set the phone inside the tray on the dashboard of his Jeep, putting it on speaker. He'd yet to tell her about the offer from Tufts and his decision to accept, and move to Boston. While the phone was still ringing, a sense of pride came over him and he smiled to himself. *I don't know where this is going. I'm still not sure where I even want it to go. I just know this is my decision to make, and I'm following my own path for the first time in as long as I can remember.*

"Professor Ben Gilsum. What are you up to, my darling? Home for the night, after a long day of preparing to enlighten a fresh crop of young minds this semester?" Angelina answered in her always cheerful tone.

"Angel, Babe, you'll never guess where I am."

Acknowledgments

Recognizing my out-of-nowhere passion to write novels, at the tender age of forty-four, would linger beyond just completing my first book, The Third King: Coronation, my wife Renee and children, Emily and Austin, continue to offer their support and encouragement. None of this would be possible without that, and I'm eternally grateful. I love you guys. Thank you for your enthusiasm and excitement. It makes a tremendous difference.

I'm especially grateful to Susan Baracco for agreeing to work with me and recognizing the potential in The Ben Gilsum Mystery Series. Collaborating with you has not only improved my writing, it's given me confidence. Thank you for making me better.

Thanks again to Jay Sennott for another fabulous cover. I send you a couple photos and a long list of crazy ideas, and you somehow translate that into exactly the image I had in mind. You're amazing, and you've made both of my books beautiful. I can't thank you enough for that.

Thank you Jim Oliveri, Ye Editor, for helping me put the finishing touches on this project, and especially for your welcome advice. Every time I work with someone new, I gain precious experience and knowledge. I appreciate your outstanding work, and your unquestionable honesty.

Finally, thank you to the wonderful cast of characters who exist in my life. You're all in here somewhere, in some form, with a different name. I'll continue to casually observe you, to be in awe of you, and to include you in my stories as much as possible with respect and admiration.

About the Author

Brian D. Campbell, author of the Ben Gilsum Mystery Series, is a Crime-Mystery author who released his first novel in the fall of 2018. The author's love of early American history is evident in the series, which is loaded with interesting historical references. Brian lives in Goffstown, New Hampshire with his lovely wife, Renee and two amazing children, Emily and Austin. The kid's involvement in field and ice hockey take the family all over the New England region. And they love it!

The first book in the Ben Gilsum Mystery Series, The Third King: Coronation, is a character-driven novel, set in the historical district of Alexandra, Virginia, with a wild series of plot twists. The characters are extremely well developed and Brian thoroughly enjoys telling their story. It's Brian's great pleasure and honor to introduce them to you and he hopes you'll enjoy reading about Ben Gilsum and his adventures!